CHAOS ON THE CANAL

INSPIRED BY ACTUAL EVENTS

GENE UPCHURCH

FIREBRAND
PUBLISHING

Firebrand Publishing publishes in a variety of print and electronic formats and by print-on-demand. For more information about Firebrand Publishing products, visit https://firebrandpublishing.com

ISBN 978-1-941907-71-9 (paperback)

ISBN 978-1-941907-72-6 (eBook)

Published by Firebrand Publishing

In loving memory

of

Merle

PART ONE

JEAN-CLAUDE QUICKLY FINISHED a lunch croissant at his desk at the Paris law firm that his father founded, handed his secretary a stack of papers to sort out and bid her farewell.

He cranked the Audi A8 and smoothly navigated the madness of Parisian traffic on his way to a four-day holiday. He pointed the big Audi toward Dijon where he would meet Madeline in a couple of hours.

This would be their first holiday together and first night as a couple. She was barely twenty-five, nearly half his age, and his heartbeat quickened at the thought of a young, classic French beauty lying next to him.

Madeline had grown up in a wealthy family with a father who was passionate about boating with a special love for barging on the *Canal du Centre* in the Burgundy region of central France. Her father had sold his barge years earlier and died the previous summer. Over a martini on their first date,

Madeline told Jean-Claude the summers on her father's barge were the happiest of her life.

With Madeline now elegantly gracing the passenger seat of the Audi, they spent a couple of hours in light and flirty conversation as they drove south into wine country.

Madeline was entertaining Jean-Claude with a funny story about shopping for clothes in Paris and was unaware they had just crossed an arched green bridge into the beautiful village of Paray-le-Monial when she looked out the windshield and sat up in her seat.

"The canal!" she shouted, hands to her face. "My beloved canal! I missed her so much!"

Jean-Claude turned onto the street fronting the historic canal, and then into a parking lot.

Lined up in front of them were seven gleaming weekender barges.

"Jean-Claude!" she exclaimed, "have you done this for me?"

Jean-Claude put his hand on her shoulder.

"The one on the far left," he said, "is ours for the next four days."

She hugged him warmly then sprang from the car and pranced to the dock where their barge awaited them.

Their gear was loaded, champagne was poured, and he expertly guided the barge into the canal for he too came from a family of boaters so the operation of the barge was no obstacle for him.

Jean-Claude planned to float through a half-dozen or so locks and past a couple of villages, perhaps as far as Génelard before mooring at a quiet spot along the canal. But the combination of delicious champagne and mutual desire forced an early mooring south of Palinges where he quickly tied up the boat and joined an eager Madeline in the barge's master suite for the night.

Afterwards, he slept blissfully and dreamed of Madeline.

Suddenly, a scream jarred him awake.

He sat upright. He looked around.

The other side of the bed was empty.

He was disoriented and frightened. He lived alone so he was unaccustomed to the noise of another person much less being awakened by screams.

Soft sunlight drifted past curtains they had neglected to close amid the passionate distractions of the night.

Then another horrifying scream.

He leapt from the tousled bed, pulled on some shorts and rushed to the bow of the barge.

Madeline was there, hands to her face.

She looked at him in terror and pointed.

He blinked in confusion, unable to process what he saw.

On the bank of the canal was an obviously dead body, the upper half of which was nearly obscured by the lush green grass and the lower half obscured by the murky brown water of the canal.

The body appeared to be that of a corpulent elderly man, a blue walking stick clutched in his right hand. A crow picked at his unseeing left eye.

A few feet away, floating face down in the canal, was the body apparently of a woman since she was wearing a dress, her hair the color of a cheap broom that had been used to sweep away vomit.

They turned away, revulsed by the grisly spectacle in the canal.

The gendarmes were alerted to this calamity by Jean-Claude on the barge's emergency radio and they quickly arrived in their little station wagons, revolving blue lights flashing in great alarm.

Jean-Claude and Madeline clutched one another and shivered in the morning chill as the gendarmes cautiously approached the scene. The officers were accustomed to dealing with pickpockets and petty thieves, but the discovery of dead bodies in their usually tranquil canal was not normal especially when it disrupted their morning croissant break.

Jean-Claude silently observed that they were hesitant to approach the scene and were clearly overwhelmed by the circumstances. One of them threw up in some bushes.

It took a few minutes, but the gendarmes gathered themselves and secured the scene with yellow tape. They then quickly moved away from the bodies as far as possible and still be professional.

They stood watch until their sergeant arrived. He was less reluctant to approach the putrid mess in the canal and stepped with great purpose to the rotting corpses where he squatted down to gaze closely at what was left of them.

After a brief investigation, the gendarme sergeant approached the shaken Jean-Claude and Madeline.

"Our investigation is obviously incomplete," he said

solemnly. "It's unclear if this was an accident or a crime. We have many questions."

He continued.

"There is no identification on these unfortunate victims, so it may take considerable time and effort to determine who they are and how they ended up face down in this lovely canal. The male victim has a pinkie ring from a British school so they may be British.

"Also, this area is a popular mooring spot for the barges, and I am wondering if they may be connected to one of them. It's the best lead I have at the moment."

The sergeant stopped for a moment, lost in his thoughts.

"You know," he said, scratching his chin, "tourists stay drunk most of the time when they're on holiday so they may have fallen overboard. And, since everyone in France and throughout the world loses patience with insufferable tourists, someone may have given them a toss."

He turned and looked over his shoulder at the scene where the bloated corpses were being dragged out of the canal and into the coroner's waiting van.

"Enjoy the rest of your holiday," the sergeant said, his gaze resting on the magnificent cleavage of the tempting young Madeline. "I'll ring you if I need you."

Jean-Claude and Madeline returned to the cabin, where he embraced his terrified lover. She shivered for a few moments, then dozed off, her breathing steady and quiet.

As the shock subsided and the effects of last night's champagne waned, his tangled brain began to remind him of the previous night in ways that didn't involve this lovely creature next to him and their amorous entanglements.

During one of the few interludes in their frantic passion, Jean-Claude had excused himself for one of his favorite rituals aboard a barge: a nighttime visit to the deck for a joyous piss into the darkness of the canal.

As he reveled in the freedom and relief of this cherished tradition, he thought he saw movement along the bank of the canal a few hundred feet from where he stood with his junk in hand.

He was unconcerned that he could be seen pissing into the canal. He peered into the darkness but couldn't tell what was happening. Was somebody dumping garbage bags into the canal? Surely not, as that is a heinous crime in this part of France and surely not to be tolerated.

He strained to see in the darkness. As his eyes adjusted, he could see what appeared to be perhaps a hotel barge which had apparently moored just ahead of them sometime after he and Madeline had stopped for the evening. As he pissed, he wondered if the passengers and crew of the hotel barge could hear him and Madeline as they flailed about in their noisy passion, then decided he didn't care.

He heard some splashing, and a few whispered words, and then nothing.

Who cares? I'm not the civil guard.

He shrugged his shoulders, finished his satisfying revelry and returned to the awaiting arms and legs of the lovely Madeline.

Now, as they lay together in the aftermath of a horrifying

morning, Madeline softly stirred from her brief nap. Her touch was irresistible, and his comfort of her terror quickly turned to passion and he became entangled with her.

As she embraced him and moved irresistibly against him, she whispered seductively to him.

He thought he would gag.

Clearly, the morning's experience had been so upsetting that she had vomited at some point. Her breath now was dreadfully vile, a toxic mixture of puke, stale champagne, the filthy herb cigarettes she craved, and her overall lack of oral hygiene since she arrived on the barge.

How could a beautiful, refined and passionate woman exhale such a horrific mess of revolting odors from her beautiful mouth that it made him wish he had a gas mask handy on the bedside table.

The effect of her noxious exhalations, however, sobered him and jolted him into a sense of clarity.

He braced for Madeline's next move and wondered if he would survive another kiss and whether she would arouse or asphyxiate him.

As he pondered the lovely but odiferous predicament of his bedmate, his tangled brain wrestled with what he might have seen hours earlier in the murky darkness of the canal.

Part Two

Dr. Peitri Bollet sat at a small sidewalk café on a side street in London's West End theater district. He sipped his dark caramel extra cream, orange latte and pondered his future.

He had a unique niche and very lucrative medical practice. He never had to cure the sniffles of obnoxious children, or give them their inoculations, stitch their wounds or explain to their frantic mothers why their poop smelled the way they did.

Instead, his only patients were the talented actors and actresses and crew members who swirled through the West End's wonderful theaters, sometimes staying for months if their show was a hit or for just a week if the reviews were bad. They were from all over the world so they had no doctor in London.

His specialty was to be on call for the sore throat of a diva, the herpes flareup of a chorus girl or the runny nose of an orchestra's violinist.

Dr. Bollet's patients came and went. But the theater bosses

knew he was reliable and would make a house call to the theater before a Saturday matinee to plug up the diarrheal guts of a leading man or eradicate the frog from the throat of a panicked soprano.

Neither his patients nor the theater bosses knew that his various cures for the sick and lame contained just a wee pinch of cut-down cocaine to make them quickly feel like the stars they were.

But as he sat at the café and sipped his complicated and costly latte, he knew a crossroad of his life was approaching like a racehorse at the finish line.

And it all depended on when a big show would close.

The defining moment of his life had come a few weeks ago. He was summoned by the producer at one of the largest theaters in town to assist with an affliction suffered by one of the young men who played a pivotal role in the hottest show in town. It was just hours before curtain.

"I'm here!" the doctor announced sternly as he arrived at the stage door where he was immediately and urgently ushered to a dressing room carrying his little black doctor's bag.

On the couch was the actor, a truly handsome young man, clearly in pain.

"Tell me what's wrong," Dr. Bollet said, frowning at the sight of someone so pitifully uncomfortable.

The actor didn't answer.

"Do you speak English?" Dr. Bollet asked, and the young actor shook his head yes.

"I'm embarrassed," the actor said in broken English but with an accent unrecognized by the doctor.

"Please don't be," Bollet said, "I'm a professional. I've seen everything."

With that, the actor pulled down his sweatpants and underwear and presented to the good doctor the largest, most infected abscess Bollet had ever seen.

And it was on the most beautiful ass the doctor had ever seen.

"I can't move like I must for the performance," the actor said, grimacing, "Every move I make is like someone is stabbing me with a scathing hot knitting needle. Please do something!"

Dr. Bollet didn't care how this affliction came to be and certainly wasn't going to ask but he knew how to fix it. He lanced it, drained it and dabbed it with a proprietary homemade mixture of cocaine, antiseptic and pain killer that he expertly whipped into a goopy paste while the young actor watched.

The doctor dabbed some of the concoction onto the beautiful ass of the actor and the expression on the face of the actor softened dramatically within moments as the pain eased. The actor pulled up his pants and made some theatrical moves, smiling as he realized that the show would go on.

"Thank you," he gushed, moving over to hug the doctor in an embrace that lasted a moment too long.

"Here," the good doctor said, holding out a tiny spoon holding a smidge of white powder. "This'll be good for you. Just a quick sniff in the nose."

The actor inhaled the power in a very practiced way.

Dr. Bollet hesitated for a moment.

"I'm in love," he said quietly, passionately, almost in a whisper.

"With who?" asked the actor, shaking his head and shrugging in confusion.

The doctor took the actor by the shoulders. He looked directly into the young man's eyes.

"You, you silly boy, with you!" the doctor exclaimed. "I've never felt this way in my life! I've seen the naked butts of thousands of patients, but yours spoke to me in a way that I've never imagined!"

The young actor, who was due in makeup in five minutes, didn't know what to do or say.

So, he said nothing.

He just stared at the doctor who looked like a love-sick sixteen-year-old cheerleader.

Bollet started blubbering, tears in his reddened eyes, his hands held dramatically to his cheeks, much like a dizzy girl in a pub who'd just met a football star.

"I know this is impossibly sudden and terribly unprofessional," Bollet said. "But I'm feeling something I have never felt, a burning in my heart and definitely a stirring in my loins."

The actor had a perplexed look on his face.

"Please come away with me!" the doctor pleaded, the urgency turning his face into a bright purple.

A knock at the door. "Makeup please!"

The young actor looked at the doctor, then at the door. He was frozen, unable to move or speak.

At least his ass felt better.

He looked back at the doctor.

"Yes," he said with a compassionate smile. "When the show's run ends."

After a wild and passionate courtship, the run of the young actor's show ended and so did Dr. Bollet's practice of medicine.

He was ready for a new life with the new love of his life. He told his relieved wife of thirty years and their confused and angry adult daughter that he was moving on. He sold his practice to his junior partners.

Dr. Bollet announced that he was to become a gentleman farmer and was off to splendid adventures in bucolic pastures and aromatic orchards with his new love.

He and his actor lover made a plan to move to the countryside in County Kent to live their expected idyllic life. They would live on a cattle farm bought by Bollet from a farmer who eagerly sold the rich and naïve doctor the whole place: a dozen beef cows, a few piles of rotting hay, a rusty tractor, sagging barn, a couple of out buildings, and a classic country house from the eighteenth century that, when viewed from the road, appeared to lean to the left.

When the lovers arrived at their new home, they paused where the driveway met the walkway.

"I cannot believe we are here together finally," he said, tears streaming down his smiling face, his arm around the thin waist of the boy actor. "I am so excited about this great new life!"

They then walked excitedly arm-in-arm up the cracked and broken sidewalk in a scene reminiscent of Dorothy and Toto prancing toward Oz on the Yellow Brick Road. They climbed the crooked and creaking front steps, kissed passionately at the unpainted threshold and swirled elegantly and triumphantly through the front door into the foyer of their dream home and their new life.

A dozen rats greeted them, momentarily stunned by the interruption, then fled frantically to their secret hiding places. Their droppings littered the foyer.

"What the fuck ...", the young actor muttered, looking at his startled lover.

The alarmed couple held hands and took tentative steps further into the house, careful to dodge the rat poo and other unknown stains on the floor. The actor removed a dainty hanky from his jacket pocket and covered his nose to block the nauseating smell of the interior of their new home, a stench similar to that of a fifteenth century pub whose men's loo hadn't been cleaned since it opened.

They moved hand-in-trembling-hand with trepidation into the main room, their eyes watering from the acrid smell of the place.

A light bulb dangled by a wire from the ceiling of the entryway as it flickered spastically. Water dripped down the stone fireplace, pooling on the rotting floor. Green moss bravely grew out of the fireplace's cracks, kept alive by the ready supply of water. The skeletal remains of a small creature were curled in a corner, its skull missing in action.

The lovers stood in stunned silence, holding each other, fearful that another step would reveal more horrors. Going upstairs was out of the question.

After a few moments of digesting the nightmare, the silence was broken.

"Oh, hell no!" shouted the actor, who wasn't acting now, snatched his hand from that of the good doctor.

The actor whipped around with great drama and without a kiss or a kiss my butt pranced out of the house and used the app on his phone to speed dial a Royal Cab to rescue him from this calamity.

Bollet tearfully pleaded with him to please stay and followed him desperately into the unkempt and overgrown yard, nearly tripping on the poorly maintained walkway, then stepping sideways to avoid a snake of some kind, pitifully sobbing and sniffling the whole way.

His soon-to-be ex-lover dismissed his pleas with a feminine wave of the arm.

The doctor was on his knees, begging the love his life to have a change of heart when the Royal Cab appeared much too quickly.

Bollet watched him go, his spirit broken, his heart ripped asunder.

The middle-finger goodbye wave from the rear window of the cab didn't help.

The ensuing days were completely miserable for Bollet.

He missed his lover desperately, and the conditions of his new home were well beneath his standards or the standards of any civilized person. The water from the spigots was brown and smelly, and the pump in the yard spewed water into the air above the pump house whenever he turned on a spigot.

In the unnerving quiet and darkness of the night, the sounds of various pests skittering around were constant, their tiny claws tip-taping on the uncarpeted floors. Sometimes during these sleepless nights, something unknown would fly by his face, creating a vortex of air that brushed his face. He was too afraid to turn on the light.

To be honest, he thought as he lay on a disgusting and now tear-stained mattress, *this place ought to be condemned.*

He self-prescribed sleep medicines and anxiety pills, but they made him throw up. The toilet was inoperable, so the contribution from his unsettled stomach only added another stink to the stank.

What I have done?!? he cried as he tried to sleep, all alone in his tilting, smelly and rat-infested home.

Even worse, he had no idea what he was doing on the farm.

He read some animal husbandry stuff on the internet, but the internet is not the real world with live animals who must be fed and cared for and often had minds of their own.

He had no idea how often they ate, what they ate, how much they ate, or where to find what they ate.

He saw other farmers putting out hay, so he did as well. The cows ate some of it but seemed to prefer the weeds and briars along the fence than the rotting mess he served them.

If cows could look at someone with contempt, that's how they looked at their new owner.

The farm quickly fell into further disrepair. The unkempt, unpainted and rotting buildings and overgrown grounds gave the place the look of total abandonment. It was a disgrace.

A few months into his new life, a passerby on the narrow rural road by Bollet's farm witnessed a startling sight.

Bollet was on foot chasing a large cow and trying to attack it with an ax. The passerby saw the doctor take a couple of wild swings at the cow, which was nimbler than its attacker, and escaped the encounter with only a scrape on its backside.

The passerby was so shocked that he reported the incident to the local constable who agreed that this was such a disturbing matter that he needed to see it for himself.

The next day, the constable drove to the Bollet farm and noticed immediately that the place was a mess and the house appeared to be leaning in an unnatural way. He pulled into the yard and looked around.

There in the field was the doctor, ax raised high, holding a furious cow by its tail.

The cow kicked and thrashed and knocked the doctor to the ground. The ax-wielding maniac recovered and started chasing the cow, which scurried back to the safety of the herd huddled together under a tree.

The constable went to the fence to take a closer look. It was obvious that some of the ax attacks had been successful because several cows had bloody scars on their necks and haunches.

He'd seen enough. But he didn't know if this was a crime or if it was within his jurisdiction.

So, he sent a most urgent message to Her Majesty's Agricultural Department, which delegated the matter to the Crown's Department of Animal Husbandry, which concluded that this was a matter for the Kingdom's Division of Animal Safety.

From there, the matter arrived on the desk of the only

employee of perhaps the most pitiful operation within all of the vaunted government of Her Majesty.

Mr. Brian Hardy.

This Hardy chap had a tiny desk in the corner of an official building occupied by government bureaucrats who had mundane but legitimate duties serving the Crown.

From his tiny desk in the corner, Mr. Hardy managed the needless and disingenuous task of governing the care of livestock who are destined to be slaughtered to satisfy the cravings of the Kingdom's citizens for steak and lamb.

In other words, the meaningless world of Mr. Hardy was to ensure the health and comfort of the country's beasts who were doomed.

"I'm the smartest person in this building," Brian would tell his colleagues in the break room. "It is a disgrace that Her Majesty's government is wasting my majestic intellect and talent on such a narrow function."

"Shut up, you idiot," was the kindest reply he usually heard from his colleagues.

He actually didn't know what he was supposed to do. He had no travel budget to check on the beleaguered livestock in the countryside nor any goals or objectives, so he sat at his little desk and waited for something to happen. No one bothered him; there was apparently no boss to give him directions, to provide him with an annual review or to give him a salary increase.

So, he sat in his corner in a state of perpetual nothingness.

Then, one day, an official document landed on his otherwise barren desk.

A constable in a nearby farming community had sounded an alarm about the mistreatment of animals.

And now it was in Brian's hands.

He immediately stood and asked for the attention of his colleagues.

"A most dramatic and urgent matter has reached my desk," he announced loudly and with great drama to a room full of people who ignored him. "I must now leave to investigate what sounds to be a horrendous situation and an affront to the decent citizens of our land."

"Shut up, you moron," came the shouted reply from across the room.

"You're an idiot!" shouted another admirer.

Brian pretended not to hear.

"I must leave now on a mission for which there is not a certain outcome and during which I will be exposed to personal danger," he said as derisive snickers could be heard. "I do not know when I will return, or if I shall return, considering the threats I may face. But it's with a full heart, immense courage and broad intellect that I depart the sanctity of this building to provide my service to the Crown."

And with that, Brian turned with a flourish and departed.

No one noticed.

———

Brian was exhausted.

He had requisitioned one of Her Majesty's government cars, an ancient tiny Citroen that was leaning ominously to port as if the left front wheel assembly might be missing some parts.

The sign on the vehicle's door identified it as part of the fleet belonging to the Crown's Women's Health Service which traveled to villages throughout the Kingdom providing prophylactics and various contraceptives to Her Majesty's friskiest commoners.

When Brian stopped for fuel or a snack, bystanders read the sign on the door and then looked at him with furrowed brow and pointed fingers, concerned that a man such as him had any responsibility whatsoever for the sexual wellbeing of the country's women.

Brian had no budget or plan for overnight lodging, so he spent a miserable night in the weary Citroen where it was impossible to get comfortable or to escape the residual rubbery odor from a box of new condoms that had been left in the back seat.

When dawn mercifully ended his sleepless night, Brian headed to the farm of a Dr. Bollet to investigate the apparently heinous behavior that was endangering livestock that were soon to be turned into hamburger.

He arrived at the farm and parked the Citroen where it coughed and rattled and shook before its tiny engine responded to the "off" switch, a puff of black smoke spitting ominously out of the tailpipe.

Brian saw a herd of cattle in the morning haze. Before he could exit the Citroen, he witnessed a most puzzling sight.

A man with an ax, presumably the farmer Bollet, was holding a cow by its nose ring and attempting to strike it. The cow swung its head back and forth, making it impossible for the man to hold the cow and swing the ax at the same time. There was much snorting and flailing and flinging of cow snot.

Brian walked to the pasture's fence.

"I say good man!" he shouted at the ax wielder. "May I have a word?"

The man apparently didn't hear Brian because he continued his spastic attack on the furious cow.

"I say again, old chap, a word please?" Brian shouted a little louder, but again was ignored.

He went to the fence's gate and entered the pasture, the first time in his life he had ever been in one.

He strode toward the ongoing confrontation between man and beast.

"I say old man!" Brian shouted, and this time the man with the ax heard him and turned, glaring at him.

"Mr. Bollet, I presume," Brian said, holding out his hand.

The gentleman farmer released the angry cow, which swung its head violently and feinted a charge at its attacker before trotting back to the herd.

"It's *Doctor* Bollet, and just who are you?" Bollet demanded breathlessly, rejecting the outstretched hand and resting the massive ax on his shoulder.

"The name is Brian Hardy," Brian said proudly, and produced a credential which the farmer ignored. "I'm from Her Majesty's government!"

"And just what do you think you're doing here?" the erstwhile farmer demanded to know.

He looked over the fence at the parked Citroen just as a wisp of steam escaped from its front hood.

"What in the world is someone from Women's Heath doing standing in my field?" the increasingly angry farmer wanted to know. "If this is about my daughter, I command you to leave immediately!"

"No, no, no!" Brian exclaimed, raising both hands in the air. "That's not it at all!"

Brian quickly told Bollet about the formal complaint which was confirmed by what he witnessed with his own eyes upon his arrival at the farm.

"This is an unacceptable way to treat your livestock," Brian insisted without actually knowing whether it was or not.

"The manner in which I decide to slaughter my herd is none of the Crown's business," Bollet said angrily.

"Wait a minute," Brian said. "You mean to tell me you were going to slaughter your cows with that ax?"

Bollet paused for a moment.

"Yes," he said reluctantly, "how else I am supposed to do it?"

Brian didn't know much, but it was obvious he knew more than Bollet about the beef industry.

"These are not barnyard chickens whose heads you can lop off as you please,"

Brian declared with indignation. "You take the doomed animals to a slaughterhouse where their sacrifice is handled with whatever dignity is possible. That's how everyone does it!"

The herd started to move toward the two men as if the cows wished to eavesdrop and determine if this stranger was another ax-wielding lunatic or perhaps had brought some fresh hay and not the dreadful crap the ax murderer fed them.

Just then, a shout from the farmhouse.

The sound of an angel.

"Daddy, oh daddy! Is everything ok?"

Bollet waved to the young woman calling to him from the porch and gave a thumbs up that he was okay.

His daughter was at the farm for a brief stay to convince her beleaguered and broken- hearted father to abandon this preposterous charade of agricultural comedy and return to London.

They had a long and unproductive talk the previous night whenshe tried to persuade him of the folly of his endeavor. She eventually surrendered to his intractable hard head and retired to a tent in the front yard to avoid a sleepless night amidst the many haunts inside her father's dreadful home.

Brian watched with enchantment as she danced lightly across the front porch until she clumsily tripped over a loose, bowed and rotten wooden floorboard on the porch of the decrepit house and plunged down the steps headfirst.

She flailed her arms and rolled ass over head onto the cracked sidewalk, her skirt flowing above her head revealing what appeared to be adult diapers, her glasses lost somewhere in the grass. Apparently, she was nearly blind as she groped around for her glasses before attempting any other efforts to recover.

Her glasses were finally located and returned to her face and she stood, returned her skirt to its rightful place and did what she could to the scraggly mess atop her head.

She gathered herself, shaking off like a freshly bathed dog, and skipped to the fence, pausing briefly to study the curious sign on the side of the beleaguered Citroen.

The farmer Bollet and Brian went to the fence to meet his daughter and introductions were made.

"Hello," she said to Brian, blushing and fluttering her eyelids like she'd seen in the movies.

Brian was captivated by what he saw.

She had thick glasses that made her slightly crossed eyeballs look the size of milky quarters sitting on a crooked witch's nose. Her hair was cut in the shape of an upside-down bowl and had the texture and color of dirty hay that had been raked up from the floor of an abandoned barn. Her hair was a mess and the rest of her was massively disheveled. It was unclear if this was her natural condition or caused by a restless night in a musty tent or her tumble down the front steps.

It mattered not.

Brian was smitten.

The sight of Brian falling in love with his daughter was confusing and painful for Dr. Bollet, and triggered in his mind an avalanche of awful memories of the poor girl's life.

He and his wife Antoinette gave up on having a child of their own. He especially had given up on children altogether with a long-range plan to leave Antoinette and do something besides listen to her constant petty bitching while he tended to the injuries and illnesses of the stars of the West End.

Antoinette worked in a medical lab as a researcher. She had

her own money and interests so he was unconcerned that he would be burdened with having to care for her in a significant way when he bid her *au revoir*.

They typically met after her workday ended (he was on call constantly) at their favorite bistro on a quiet side street on the edge of the West End. It was convenient for him if he was called to duty, and he didn't care if it was convenient for Antoinette. It wasn't, but it was the one thing she didn't whine about.

"Darling," she said one evening as they sipped cognac after another light dinner that was absent of any conversation whatsoever. "I've come across something that I'd like to discuss."

Dr. Bollet was barely listening as he read the silly biographies of the actors in the Playbill of the West End's hottest new show.

"What is it, dear?" he replied, his attention riveted on a particular young actor who appeared to be captivating.

Antoinette laid a computer printout on the table. It was in a foreign language.

"What is this?" he asked impatiently.

"Sweetheart, I had it translated," she said, excitement rising in her voice. "I found it at work while researching a rare disease in Baltic countries that may actually be the bubonic plague or something like it. It's fascinating!"

He looked at Antoinette with concern to hear that she was fumbling around with a potential plague. His brow was furrowed and his impatience rising as he hoped his medical beeper would soon frantically call him away from whatever was happening at his table. He wondered if he should put on a mask.

"What does this have to do with us?" he asked.

Antoinette sighed deeply, then went on to explain to the doctor that this was an online pamphlet for an illegal orphanage in rural Lithuania.

"I've heard of Lithuania and generally know where it is," Bollet said untruthfully.

Antoinette went on to explain that the pamphlet was vague and full of innuendo, especially when translated into English which made it almost indecipherable. But she had done some checking and learned that this place made it simple and easy to adopt a Lithuanian orphan and return home to wherever you lived with a fresh, new child. No muss, no fuss, and all completely illegal if you had cash and lots of it.

Antoinette sat up straight in her chair.

"I want a baby," she said without emotion. "And this is where we're going to get one."

He wasn't sure what happened or how Antoinette made this happen, but very soon they were in a rented Range Rover on their way to Lithuania on an exhausting, two-day trip across northern Europe.

Antoinette had made all the arrangements and sent a large sum of money to the officials at the orphanage, receiving a verbal promise that everything would work out just fine.

They arrived at the orphanage late on a snowy afternoon. Antoinette leaped from the Range Rover and dashed into the office, desperate to see her new child before the office closed for the day.

Dr. Bollet exited the car, stretched his legs casually and followed her in.

They were led by a nun into a large nursery filled with

dozens of cribs and changing tables and all the equipment needed to support tiny orphans.

It was completely silent.

They both had expected a lively, exciting room buzzing noisily with crying and cooing babies and nurses busily changing diapers, burping the little ones and cleaning up their spit and poo.

There was none of that.

Bollet and Antoinette looked at each other, slightly alarmed.

"Where are all the babies?" Antoinette asked the nun.

"They've all been adopted," the nun replied, smiling excitedly. "We have but one left. Yours!"

She held out her arm elegantly and led them to the corner of the room.

There, laying in a crib, was their child.

"Uff," Bollet grunted and turned pale.

Antoinette looked away for a moment to gain her composure, then looked again at the child in the crib as the nun smiled like a used car salesman trying to unload a lemon with sawdust in the transmission.

In a world where almost every baby is cute beyond words, the child in this crib was as unattractive as any either of them had ever seen.

"She was left on the doorstep of a firehouse in the next village," the nun said. "She was in a wire chicken basket wrapped in a thin blanket. Whoever left her put her basket right in the middle of the driveway. The firemen didn't know she was there until they almost flattened her on the way to a fire."

The nun's dramatic tale continued.

"They didn't flatten her, thank God, but swooped up the chicken basket and the little girl and took her with them to the fire where she stayed in the fire truck. After that fire, they went directly on another call to help a man who was choking on a piece of antelope meat, so it was a couple of hours before they returned to the firehouse."

The nun went on to explain that the child was nearly unconscious from hunger and exposure when everyone was safely back at the firehouse. The firemen, being great guys, took the child in, warmed her up and sent for the proper food and clothing which was quickly brought to the firehouse by one of their wives.

"When the wife arrived with the proper supplies for an infant," the nun continued, "she actually was thinking of bringing the orphan into her own home to raise with her other six children. She was excited about the prospects of another child without the distasteful mess of conceiving it or the burden of bearing a seventh herself.

"But one peek at the child in the chicken basket made her change her mind, and that's why she's here."

Bollet and Antoinette looked at each other, concern and possible regret on both their faces.

The nun continued in broken English.

"She had a rough birthing," she said. "It is normal for them to look disfigured this early in their life. She'll grow out of it."

Antoinette's features softened as her maternal instincts clicked into gear, a soft smile appeared on her face.

'I love her."

Oh my god, Bollet thought, wisely keeping his thoughts private.

"Does she have a name? asked Antoinette.

"Yes," said the nun. "Her name is Ugnė, which means 'fire' in our language. The firemen named her."

Bollet snorted and thought, again wisely to himself, that her evil schoolmates would call her Ugly Ugnė.

Antoinette looked at her husband.

"We've come a long way, dear," she said, "and this pitiful child needs a loving home. I cannot imagine leaving her here in this empty room with no one to love her."

Bollet remained silent.

"We'll take her," Antoinette said firmly to the nun as if she was buying a pound of salmon from a fishmonger. "And we'll call her Helga. Ugnė simply will not do."

"Very well," said the nun. "I'll finalize the papers."

Somewhere during the complex transaction, a guy in a little back room at the orphanage who created the fake passports for the adopted children confused the translation or just screwed up.

So, the Bollets trekked back home to Great Britain with their illegal, expensive and quite unattractive baby. They crossed the borders of four countries, each time producing a fake British passport.

And each time the border patrol admitted into their country a tiny child named Hilary.

Part Three

It was the same conversation every night at dinner.

"When the hell are you gonna' move out, you asshole?" Brian's father would yell at him, pounding the handle of his knife on the wooden table, shaking the water glasses.

Brian still lived with his parents. He was forty-five years old and still slept in his childhood bed in his childhood room. The faded posters of Barry Manilow, Donnie Osmond and Farrah Fawcett were still affixed to the walls where he pinned them up decades ago.

His mum washed his undies and fixed his meals, including a hot breakfast every day before he departed for his meaningless job serving the Kingdom.

"I mean, for god's sake, son, you're a grown man," his father would moan. "Are you gay?"

So now was the big moment. He looked solemnly at his parents.

"I've met a woman. We're to be married," he said.

His father sat in stunned silence, dropping his cutlery to the floor. His mum cried.

It was not easy getting to this point, but here he was. Finally.

The courtship had been arduous. Hilary was reluctant to be married to Brian or anyone else because of the demands of her career.

"I am the smartest person in my company," she told Brian repeatedly. "My subordinates demand my constant attention and thrive on my direction. My superiors would fail without my knowledge and expertise. The company would cease to exist without my steady hand.

"I do not have the time, energy or desire to be a wife to a husband."

This kind of talk excited Brian immensely.

So, he told her how smart he was, and they had a contentious debate about who was the smartest. Over several months they assembled a tortured arrangement for their life together that included no vacations, no shared beds in their new joint home and a completely sexless life together.

"Sounds good to me," Brian said as they sealed the deal with a handshake.

"Whatever," Hilary said.

The life of Brian and Hilary went along about as you would expect it until one day when the phone rang on Brian's little desk for the first time in three years.

A complaint had been filed about a farmer in southeast England who was accused of abusing his flock of goats and sheep. As before, Brian announced proudly to his colleagues that he had been summoned to do important work on behalf of Her Majesty and he would be gone for an unknown period of time.

His announcement was met with hissing and vulgarities shouted in his direction.

Two days later, he was at the farm and announced that an investigation had been launched in response to a complaint.

The farmer seemed unworried.

"Have a look around your honor, I think you'll find every-thing is in order," the farmer said with a wry smile.

Brian's review revealed nothing out of the ordinary, but he still had little clue about what he should be looking for. He returned to the sheep barn where the farmer awaited him.

"Everything seems to be in order," Brian announced. "I am perplexed by the reason for the complaint."

"That's great, mate," the farmer said. "Now, I've got a ques-tion for you."

The farmer looked at Brian, a big grin on his face.

"Not sure exactly how to ask it, so I'll just ask it gently and hope you get what I'm asking," he said.

Brian shrugged and nodded.

The farmer continued.

"So, mate, have you ever, how can I say this politely, had your way with a sheep?"

Brian's jaw dropped and his face turned bright red. He shuffled like a schoolboy at his first dance.

The farmer studied his reaction.

"You must be a city boy," the farmer concluded. "This is how all the boys in these parts learn how to become a man. And the sheep don't mind, or at least they don't seem to."

Brian's brain short-circuited.

Was this guy actually suggesting he have relations with one of the farm animals?

He didn't know what to say.

"Let's give 'er a try, whatdya say old mate," the farmer said, slapping Brian on the back.

"All the other investigators over the years gave it a go. Why shouldn't you?"

Brian thought for a moment and concluded that this was a convincing argument because he certainly wanted to be like everyone else.

The farmer who went to a nearby stall and returned with a huge sheep that had a disinterested look on its face. The sheep expertly backed up to Brian in a well-practiced move.

Before he knew it, Brian's pants were around his ankles. But nothing happened.

In Brian's loins, that is. He couldn't get it going.

"Now!" shouted the farmer.

From behind a stall door jumped one of Brian's colleagues from his office in London, a Polaroid camera in hand.

He snapped a quick photo and ran from the barn.

In less than sixty seconds, the Polaroid revealed a clear photo showing the shocked faces and naked rear ends of both Brian and the sheep. Thankfully, the angle of the photo did not allow for the revelation of the flaccid nature of Brian's failed manhood.

The photo was mailed anonymously to The London Times with a note alleging that the photographed bureaucrat who was responsible for the comfort and safety of the Kingdom's slaughter-bound livestock was, in fact and without doubt, actually consorting with them in a perverted way.

The Times ran the story without doing a lot of checking or reporting and published the photo after pixilating the faces of both Brian and the sheep.

"Mr. Hardy."

Brian looked up from his desk. Three men in suits stood before him.

"Yes, how may I serve you?" Brian asked. "Are there farm animals who need my attention?"

The men looked at each other. *You've got to be kidding. What a pervert.*

One of the men laid the morning's Time on Brian's desk, opened to the page with the photo of Brian's flabby butt and his date.

"Sir," the man said. "This department has been eliminated. We have looked diligently, but there is no other position for you in Her Majesty's government."

"But I was clearly set up," Brian said, standing up. "The whole thing was an ambush."

"Mr. Hardy, photos do not lie. Please gather your things. We'll escort you to the door."

All of Brian's stuff fit into a single plastic grocery bag provided by the men in suits. And, with that, Brian was led to the door amid the hurrahs and cheers of everyone on the office floor.

"Fuck off, asshole!" came a shout as the door closed behind him.

Part Four

He was too ashamed to tell Hilary that he'd been fired for having a sheep for a mistress, so he pretended to go to work for several weeks. She never asked about his work, so he was never required to lie to her about his whereabouts or activities.

Most days he sat on a bench in the park. On a good day, an unlucky soul would stop for a rest on the bench and get a long lecture from Brian about some inane subject. Of course, it didn't take Hilary long to figure out that Brian was jobless.

And it didn't take much longer than that for Hilary's bosses to figure out that she was blowing smoke about how smart she was.

It became obvious when her company recruited some newbies from one of the universities at Oxford who actually were smart. Hilary kept correcting them in meetings and in emails when she was absolutely wrong about everything. The bosses did some checking and discovered that Hilary's ill-informed bluster had cost the company millions of pounds over the years. She was led from the building, tears of anger welling behind her bug-eyed glasses.

After painfully confessing to each other that they were both unemployed, they sat around for a few weeks trying to decide what to do with their lives and their pitiful attempt at a marriage.

"Hilary, dear," Brian said one morning, breaking the tradition of silence at their table, "whatever shall we do?"

Hilary declined to put down the newspaper as if blocking the view of the other person at the table would also drown out the intolerable droning coming from that other person.

"Seriously, Hilary, we can't just sit here in silence," he declared as he poured another spot of tea. "We need to live our lives. Do something interesting."

She continued to hide behind her newspaper, so he was basically talking to the back page of The London Times. Where there was a full color advertisement. For an adventure unlike anything either of them had ever experienced.

It was an advertisement for a hotel barge in France.

It was named *The Renaissance*.

An audience of ten fellow passengers with whom to share their massive knowledge and intellect was exhilarating for Brian and Hilary as the elegant and well-appointed *Renaissance* cast off for a week of winding its way through one of the ancient canals of central France offering memorable scenery and delectable French cuisine.

The first night was splendid for the passengers with an elegant five-course meal served on the outside deck under a French sky filled with French stars.

It was not so splendid for Brian and Hilary.

They were consumed with dread and angst at the highly negative and barely tolerable aspect of sharing a room with each other for the first time in their marriage. They had requested separate cabins on the *Renaissance* but there were only six and none were vacant. Then they requested separate beds arranged as far apart as possible.

When they were delivered to their cabin upon arrival at the *Renaissance,* they were dismayed to find a king bed in a small cabin and were informed by the crew that no other option or configuration was available.

They sighed. This was a major and unpleasant departure from their home where they each had their quarters on opposite ends of their brownstone and had never seen each other anywhere close to a state of undress.

This was a venture into the marital unknown. Their only options were to leave and cancel the trip or soldier on. Unable to resist the siren call of a week with a captive audience with whom to share their superior intelligence, they agreed to soldier on and make the best of it.

They were quiet at dinner while the other guests chatted lively and drank heavily. As the delicious and voluminous amounts of wine took their toll, the other guests shamelessly flirted with their spouses and engaged in unabashed flirtation with other spouses. It was a boozy, loose start to the cruise, and Brian and Hilary had no idea what was going on.

At the end of the evening, everyone bid a slurred good night and lurched to their cabins with their own drunk spouses.

Brian and Hilary remained on deck as long as possible, the awkwardness of what lay ahead hanging over them like a thick fog. They did everything they could to postpone the trip down the stairs to their cabin until the crew said it was time for everyone to be safely stowed away for the night.

They agreed ahead of time there would be no lights. Complete darkness except for perhaps a dim nightlight to aid with any nocturnal trips to the toilette.

Brian changed in the bathroom into a full fleece pajama set, including wool socks, and then felt his way through the darkness to the bed where he crawled under the covers, drawing them up to his many chins.

Hilary didn't change and a moment later crept toward the bed wearing her dinner clothes. In the total darkness, she had no idea where Brian was. Suddenly, she was on top of him, unaware in the darkness that she had fumbled onto his side of the bed.

"Oh, Hilary," Brian said breathlessly, "this is a surprise!"

Hilary froze. She lay still for a moment, unsure what to do. The evil nuns didn't teach this at Catholic school.

They had never touched each other, much less lain on top of one another. They had never kissed until just now when Brian's grotesque lips groped awkwardly through the darkness until his found hers. She felt a bulge where none should be, and a hand was on her ass where none should be.

And it felt *good*.

The next few minutes were a calamitously noisy spectacle as many of the passengers and crew of the majestic *Renaissance* were treated to the moaning and groaning and caterwauling of a middle-aged couple trying to figure out where all the parts go. They loudly and profanely bossed each other around, even though neither knew what they were doing.

This is somewhat better than a sheep, Brian mused to himself as he groped previously undiscovered parts of Hilary's anatomy with the intensity of a Mount Everest expedition.

Any of the passengers who slept through the banging and yelling of the clumsy mating up to this point were awakened when the encounter reached its nauseating conclusion accompanied by unashamed but disgraceful shouts of *"Holy shit, baby!"*, *"Bring it, big boy!"*, and *"Lemme have it all!"* that could be heard throughout the dignified *Renaissance* and probably by some of the astonished villagers who were nowhere near the boat.

At one point, the other passengers who were eavesdropping were startled to hear a loud thump, a shriek of pain or delight (it was impossible to tell the difference) and the sound of overturned furniture.

It sounded more like a bare-fisted fight at a biker bar than a session of bedroom passion. Several passengers contemplated knocking on the lovers' door to see if assistance was required, but ultimately decided to leave it alone.

A few hours later, now in the middle of the night, the passengers were awakened again to a methodical banging. Some arose from their beds concerned there had been a collision on the canal, or thieves were trying to gain entry to the barge. They returned to their beds when the banging stopped amidst loud groans indicating a collision of a different kind had just occurred – again.

"How was your night?' one of the passengers sarcastically asked Brian the next morning as the stewardess serving orange juice giggled and blushed. "I don't know about you, but I didn't get much sleep."

"I slept just fine," Brian said, his nose in the air. "Why would you ask?"

A slight smile crept onto his face as he remembered fondly that the passion between him and his insatiable wife reached such a frenzied peak that they fell off the bed, overturning the bedside table and knocking their water glasses and a table lamp onto the floor. The collision shattered the glasses and a light bulb, hence the loud thump, shriek and other assorted and disturbing noises heard throughout the barge.

Hilary soon emerged from the downstairs cabin, a slight grin also on her lips. Her hair was in its usual state of askew wildness, a blush on her cheeks and robed in the same wrinkled clothes in which she dined the previous evening. One of the sleeves, however, was ripped and there was a stain of some sort on a pant leg.

"Good morning, dear," she said.

"Good morning, honey," he replied.

Brian then tapped his water glass with a butter knife to get everyone's attention and announced to the passengers who were assembled for their peaceful breakfast that he had decided the topics of conversation for the group when they convened for lunch and dinner during their week together.

It was a complex list of world and military issues as well as obscure history.

"I urge you to spend the day preparing lest you lack the ability or knowledge to partake in the upcoming discussions," Brian said sternly to his barge mates.

And that's how it went all week.

Lunch on the final day was lavishly presented to the passengers on the outside deck on a sun-splashed afternoon with a deliciously chilled local chardonnay and a light pinot served in large quantities to wash down the chef's magical creations.

Brian, sitting at the head of the table as usual, provided his sixth lunch lecture of the week. He spoke throughout lunch, pausing only to cram some French cuisine into his mouth and swallow without tasting or chewing, hesitant to pause lest one of his barge mates might have something to say.

The issue for discussion was the challenge faced by the British Navy a century ago when it attempted to discover the Northwest Passage and why so many attempts failed.

Brian offered his views and was abruptly interrupted by his wife, who threw her napkin down and begged to differ. The two then began a loud debate with neither backing down.

"Will you two just shut the fuck up!" one exasperated fellow passenger finally shouted, interrupting the lively debate. "We've been listening to your shit for a solid week now! Just shut the fuck up!"

Brian and Hilary looked at each other astounded that their

brilliance and insights appeared to be unwelcomed and unappreciated. But at least they shut the fuck up.

On their way home, they analyzed the week, including the confrontation with the other passenger.

"I thought it was great," Brian said. "We were able to speak to a small group of strangers for a week and share our knowledge. I liked the small vessel because there was no place for anyone to hide."

Hilary nodded in agreement, but she was studying an online travel guide and not listening at all to what her husband was saying.

"Listen to this, dear," she said to him and read the description and itinerary of another barge, this time on a smaller boat. "I think it would enhance our experience if we can share our vast intellect in a more intimate setting. You can talk to three people, and I can talk to three as well. At the same time! How glorious!"

Within minutes, they were booked for a week-long voyage.

Aboard the *Princesse de la Gourmandise*.

PART FIVE

THE LAUGHTER from the barge could be heard through the open windows of the tidy beige villas in the little town of St.-Léger-sur-Dheune which clung to the side of the *Canal de Centre.*

The local folks were accustomed to the sounds from the canal and, over the years, their lives had become synced with the comings and goings of the slow-moving barges that crept past their homes and occasionally moored near the green bridge that connected their little world to everywhere else.

In a different era, the barges hauled goats and coal from one end of the region to the other. The goats were slaughtered and the coal was burned, all part of the thriving commerce of central France at that time. The canals were built during Napoleon's reign to facilitate the efficient movement of troops who crowded onto barges that were towed by mules on well-worn paths alongside the canal. These paths were now paved so that arrogant

French bicyclists could hurtle through the countryside on their fancy bikes and harass the ignorant tourists who didn't know what was going on.

The barges were now elegant floating hotels that hauled wealthy tourists who spent thousands of Euros per week to gawk at the farmers and villagers along the canal and tour the wineries and other attractions on the fifty-mile route. The locals laughed at the dumb tourists who spent so much money and time traveling at two knots through the canal when they could see all they wished in an automobile in half a day.

On this breathtakingly beautiful French evening, the barge named *Princesse de la Gourmandise* was moored along a grassy strip that separated St.-Léger-sur-Dheune from the canal.

The cruise was nearing its end, and the passengers were on their second round of cocktails and enjoying the experience. Nobody had to drive anywhere, and the farthest anyone had to travel tonight was down a short flight of stairs to the luxurious suites awaiting them below deck.

One of the suites was empty so if one of the couples had a drunk fight or needed to escape from a noisy snorer, the crew had left the door unlocked and the young captain, with a laugh, cautioned against illicit rendezvouses. The passengers looked at one another as if such a thing was remotely possible, then simultaneously burst out laughing at the outrageousness of the idea.

Their laughter was contagious, and the local villagers wondered what was so funny.

There were six of them, all from the United States, and five crew members from around the world all under the age of twenty-five except for the classically trained French chef who now was putting the final touches on a sauce he had specially created for the roast duck that was finishing in the oven.

Three bottles of Burgundian wine were already breathing on the outdoor patio where the happy passengers would dine tonight, a classic white and a couple of reds. It was likely that others would be uncorked as the evening progressed.

They drank their cocktails, snacked on hors d 'oeuvres that included a freshly made paté the chef bought this afternoon at a market in St.-Léger-sur-Dheune after the barge arrived. They laughed joyously as they relived their adventures of the day.

"May I come aboard?"

The laughter stopped as the entire population of the barge whipped their heads toward the bank of the canal.

A gendarme sergeant resplendent in his opulent uniform stood in the grass at the end of the gangplank.

He was exhausted. He had tracked this barge nearly the entire length of the *Canal du Centre* certain that its occupants held the secret to the atrocity near Palinges. It shouldn't have been this difficult considering the barge cruised at two knots. But it was.

He held out his badge.

"Captain, I have the most urgent business. May I come aboard?" he asked.

The young captain was French and had shared with some of the passengers his background and experience. To be so young, he had accomplished much in the complicated world of ships and sailing and possessed the poise and demeanor of a real leader. It was actually surprising that someone with his qualifications was taking a turn commanding a barge that barely moved, but it was clear that he was delighted with where he was in his life. And it was obvious to all that the attractive blonde hostess who was barely twenty spent more nights in his cabin than in the one she was assigned to share with the barge's other hostess.

"What is your business?" the young captain asked the sergeant.

"I have questions for your crew and passengers regarding missing persons," the sergeant replied.

The mood on the deck was suddenly solemn.

The passengers looked at one another. No one changed their expression. Then they looked at their young captain, waiting for him to reply to the sergeant.

The captain looked at his passengers with resignation, shrugged his shoulders and motioned the sergeant aboard.

"My apologies for interrupting or delaying your dinner," he said, looking at the elegantly prepared table that awaited the diners.

The chef emerged from the cabin, hands on hips, rage in his eyes. The roast duck had to be served promptly and at the perfect temperature. Timing was everything! Any delay was an outrageous affront to his effort!

The sergeant looked at the small gathering, still standing with cocktails in hand, and told them what had been found on the banks of the canal.

The passengers had gathered earlier that week in the lobby of a prestigious hotel in the historic downtown area of Dijon. This was the gathering point where a van and driver would collect them for the short trip to the canal, the first step of their long-awaited barge cruise.

As each couple entered the lobby, they were excitedly asked, "Are you on *the Princesse de la Gourmandise*?"

If the answer was yes, introductions were made, and inquiries made about where everyone lived.

Judgments were made immediately. Only four couples would be on the barge, so it would be intimate.

The British couple was the last to arrive. The male partner of the pair limped into the lobby with a blue cane in one hand and a small satchel in the other. His wife trailed him, straining to maneuver two enormous rolling suitcases.

"I must have the front seat," the British man demanded loudly in a thick brogue before saying good morning or introducing himself to anyone. "As you can see, I have an affliction and simply cannot get in and out of the rear of any vehicle."

The other passengers looked at one another, shoulders slumped with disappointment. *So, he's gonna be one of those,* they all thought.

After a few awkward moments, he finally introduced himself to his fellow passengers as Brian and allowed his wife, Hilary, to introduce herself.

Brian and Hilary immediately began jabbering about their previous travels and shared their worry that *the Princesse de la Gourmandise* would not measure up. They talked at the same time and argued with each other about details from other travels.

After what seemed an interminable wait, the driver from the barge arrived and everyone excitedly made their way to the van where the driver hoisted Brian's crippled body into the coveted front seat.

The thirty-minute drive seemed like two hours as Brian and Hilary continued a non-stop barrage about a particular obsession with a barge named *Renaissance*, which Hilary pronounced *Ray-NAY-Saunce* in her irritating thick accent. It was *Ray-NAY-Saunce* this and *Ray-NAY-Saunce* that with Brian frequently interrupting to add commentary or to correct Hilary until the van mercifully arrived at the canal where their floating hotel for the next six nights awaited them.

The passengers met the crew and briefly freshened up, eager to get back to the upper deck where a marvelous party had been prepared to celebrate their arrival. There was a safety briefing by the captain and the bar was opened.

And then it continued.

More jabbering from the Brits about their beloved *Ray-NAY-Saunce* now that they'd had five minutes to compare it to the *Princesse de la Gourmandise*. Their current vessel was smaller than the marvelous *Ray-NAY-Saunce* and they wondered how such a small kitchen could meet their sophisticated needs that had been so marvelously satisfied aboard the magnificent *Ray-NAY-Saunce*.

"I must sit at the head of the table," Brian announced when they were called to dinner which was to be served outside at a table that had been beautifully prepared. "I need extra room because of my affliction, and this must be the case at every meal."

Hilary added, "The people on the *Ray-NAY-Saunce* were so supportive of Brian. They were happy for him to sit at the head of the table."

The other passengers gave each other *the* side eye and shook their heads at the prospects of six days of this crap.

It got worse.

Visits to every winery and museum slowed to a glacial pace and were altered to accommodate Brian's swollen and twisted legs including arrangements for a staff person to follow him around with a folding chair so he could sit when the host would pause the tour briefly to explain something important.

At one of Burgundy's most prestigious wineries, the lovely and intelligent and interesting hostess could barely get a word in because Brian thought the group wanted to hear about how this winery compared to one that he and his witch-faced wife had visited in New Zealand.

"I want to hear what *she* has to say, not you!" one of his fellow passengers finally snapped at Brian, who appeared to not understand what the fuss was about.

Nevertheless, the van ride back to the barge was made in icy silence.

The last straw came at dinner that night when Hilary stood at the dinner table to make an announcement.

"Everyone's departure time on the final morning will be four hours earlier than planned because Brian and I wish to catch an earlier train to return to the luxurious comfort and separate bedrooms of our flat in London," she pronounced.

The other passengers realized immediately that Hilary's proclamation meant they all would unnecessarily rise pre-dawn to accommodate the Brits and then wait around for hours and hours for their own transport.

"Oh, hell no!" shouted Leeza, one of the passengers from North Carolina, a serrated steak knife gripped tightly in her right hand and, in her left, a vodka martini the remnants of which she threw into the shocked face of Hilary.

Leeza continued to make her point.

"We will NOT be inconvenienced by you inconsiderate ass wipes just so you can get home a little earlier than planned!" she yelled. "We have been patient while you have commandeered this whole trip and we're sick of it. What is WRONG with you?"

Silence fell upon the barge.

Something had to be done.

Trey and Gregg, friends from North Carolina and on the *Princesse de la Gourmandise* with their wives, one of whom had just flung the dregs of a martini into the face of Hilary, moved to a far corner of the deck, freshened their drinks, clinked their glasses in the customary fashion and agreed on a plan to be implemented the next evening.

They told no one.

It was elegant in its simplicity.

Trey suffered occasionally from kidney stones, the pain of which can be compared to a woman's protracted labor of overweight triplets gripping sewing needles in their tiny newborn baby hands as they emerged from unspeakable parts of their mother's anatomy. His travels always included an assortment of medicines to help him deal with the excruciating pain of an attack should one occur. The most powerful tool in his pain-killing arsenal was a thirty pack of five hundred milligram codeine tablets.

The plan, such as it was, was to slip the Brits enough codeine so they'd stay in their cabin for a couple of days, shut the fuck up and leave everyone alone. Neither Trey nor Gregg had any idea how many tablets it would take so they swore to one another that they would carefully monitor the dispensing of the medicine.

The next evening was lovely. As a full moon climbed above the trees next to the canal, Trey and Gregg assumed the roles of gracious hosts, bartenders, and amateur unlicensed pharmacists. They served drinks and wine to the Brits who drank them with gusto, oblivious to the devilish contents of their concoctions.

"Hey," Brian said to his bartenders, "these drinks are really delicious, better than usual. I must have the recipe."

"Absolutely," Trey said winking at Gregg, "let me write it down for you."

Unsurprisingly, Trey and Gregg fell drunk and naturally lost track of who had served what to Brian and Hilary.

Trey and Gregg stepped aside to confer.

Trey inspected the box of codeine.

It was empty.

They looked at each other, somewhat concerned.

Thirty tablets in the flabby British bellies.

"Oops," Trey said, eyebrows raised.

"Oh dear," Gregg said, his words slightly slurred so it sounded like he said "Odor."

At that moment, Brian raised his hand at his usual seat at the head of the table as if to be recognized for a speech.

"Mah olip guj xirt sigl," he shouted defiantly and slammed his hand on the table, overturning a half-filled wineglass, sloshing its contents onto the fine clothes of his annoyed table mates.

He tried to spew out some additional gibberish but his eyes suddenly went blank and his mouth stopped working except to expel a thimbleful of vomit followed by a brief gagging spell.

As the other passengers held their collective breath at what calamity might occur next, Brian plummeted with great drama face down into the puff pastry that had taken all afternoon to be baked by the chef who would be monstrously displeased that his magnificent creation was now the resting place of Brian's snout.

The other passengers froze at the sight of this spectacle.

Hilary reached out to comfort her dear husband who was obviously having a spot of trouble. But her brain was so short-circuited that she lovingly caressed not her distressed husband but the table's elegant floral centerpiece before collapsing back into her chair and nearly sliding onto the floor, a long thread of filthy spittle dangling from her mouth.

She muttered something incomprehensible about the *Re-nay-saunce*, but she only got as far as *Re-nay* before her eyes rolled back in her head and she spoke no more.

"What a mess," Trey said quietly to Gregg. They both shrugged their shoulders as if to say, *"Oh well."*

The rest of the group looked knowingly at one another and slinked off to the relative sanity of their cabins, leaving the British couple alone in their tortured slumber.

Trey and Gregg also went below and waited a few minutes before returning to the upper deck.

The codeine couple hadn't moved and the crew apparently had gone into hiding without clearing the table which was understandable considering the unconscious obstacles blocking their way.

Trey and Gregg looked at each other.

Their plan had worked, or at least it seemed so. It was clearly going to be a while, if ever, before Brian and Hilary uttered any more tiresome drivel.

But they hadn't really thought through the consequences of, let's say, killing them.

Brian hadn't moved since face planting into the chef's beloved pastry. Trey put two fingers to Brian's clammy, damp neck but he didn't really know what he was doing. He didn't feel a pulse but wasn't entirely sure.

"I've never been around that many dead people except for the old farts who eat lunch together every Friday at our club, but these two look pretty dead to me," Gregg said, glaring at Trey. "I didn't sign on for this shit. "

"You can count as good as me," Trey replied impatiently. "Whose idea was it to hand out dangerous narcotics like Halloween candy? That whole box of pills would kill a fat hog."

They paused for a moment to laugh at that comparison.

"I wonder if the bar is still open," Gregg said, looking longingly at the liquor cabinet in the cabin."

"C'mon man, we gotta clean this mess up, if you know what I mean," Trey said.

"I never know what you're talking about," Gregg said. "And another thing. If you write one of your bullshit, nonsense stories about this, please don't use my real name. In fact, leave me out of it altogether."

Trey ignored Gregg's demand as he spotted Gregg's iPad on the table, sparking an idea.

"I need you to google how to dispose of overdose victims," Trey said.

"I would be happy to," Gregg said, not thinking clearly that such a search could land him in prison. "But I don't have a connection. Haven't since we left home. I save a lot of money with my wireless plan, but it doesn't work beyond my front yard."

"But you've been staring at it for nearly a week," Trey said. "What've you been looking at?"

"Solitaire!"

"Good lord," Trey said. "Grab a fat arm and let's get these pigs outta here."

It took them a half hour to drag the Brits down the gangplank and through the darkness of the warm French night about a hundred yards on the towpath behind where the *Princesse de la Gourmandise* was moored. Brian was the most difficult because he weighed as much as an elephant seal and was about as flabby.

They dragged his lumpy carcass as far as they could but couldn't get him all the way in the canal. Hilary's small body was easier to dump in the canal.

At dawn, the captain of the *Princesse de la Gourmandise* started her small diesel engine and slowly moved from her mooring on to her next stop.

———

The sergeant continued his questions.

"So, no one noticed they were missing. Is that what you're saying?"

He looked at the passengers, and then at the crew.

Everyone nodded in agreement.

He turned to the captain.

"And you acknowledge, sir, that you were moored very near where we found their bodies a few days ago?"

The captain nodded in agreement.

"That's correct. We always moor at that spot. The company has an arrangement with the village of Palinges that compensates it for allowing us to spend the night," the captain said with a shrug. "That's simply how it works."

"Do you have surveillance cameras?" the sergeant asked.

"Why, of course," replied the captain.

Trey and Gregg gasped and tried not to faint.

"Excellent," said the sergeant.

"But they don't work," the captain said. "Something about the Bluetooth link. We've never been able to get them to work. We don't even know what Bluetooth is."

The sergeant's shoulders slumped.

Suddenly the French chef burst through the door of the cabin and onto the deck, a huge knife in his hand.

'MY FUCKING DUCK MUST BE SERVED NOW!" he shouted, glaring at the sergeant.

"I'm afraid you are inconveniencing my passengers and must go," the captain said quietly. "We have no information that will help you. We don't know what happened."

Leeza said, "I've got a great duck joke that I'll tell when everybody calms the fuck down. But I'll need two more glasses of wine if I'm gonna tell it right."

The sergeant, however, was not finished.

"A final question, then I'll leave you," he said. "Were they drinking heavily when you last saw them?"

"Everybody on this barge is a heavy drinker," the captain replied with a wry smile. "I've never seen anything like it. These people are professional drinkers, especially the two couples from North Carolina. We've had to resupply liquor and wine twice already and the voyage is only a week. But that's beside the point. When I last saw the victims, they had passed out on the deck. From there, who knows?"

The sergeant nodded respectfully to the young captain and, in doing so, clearly acknowledged that nothing further could be accomplished by continuing to pester these nice people.

"I will leave you now and disturb you no further," he said to the group as the chef glared at him. "But before I take my leave, may I please be allowed to use your guest toilette?"

"We don't have one," the captain said in the classic impatient French manner, with lots of shoulder shrugging and hand waving. "But there's an empty cabin. You may use that."

The captain motioned to the stairs leading down to the guest cabins.

The sergeant bowed from the waist in gratitude and went downstairs, entering the first cabin he came to. It was obvious this wasn't the vacant one because there was luggage, but he decided against wandering around to find the correct one.

He went into the elegant and well-appointed toilette, which was larger than the one in his apartment. He looked longingly at the comfortable toilet seat and thought about how wonderful it would be to spend an hour there with a good book.

But obviously there was no time for such tempting pleasures of the bowels. He needed to take care of his business and leave these people alone.

As he zipped his trousers from a satisfying piss, his eye fell to an object in the small brass trash can next to the toilet.

He bent down for a closer look.

"These people are mine now," he growled to himself, followed by a maniacal chuckle as he slipped the object into his jacket pocket, returned to the main cabin and bid a good night to the restless group on deck.

The lieutenant of the gendarmerie station looked at his sergeant with the weary dejection of someone who had not seen everything but had seen too much.

"No," he said emphatically, a deep sigh punctuating his message. "You've spent too much time on a couple of stoned, dead Brits who mixed so much whisky, wine and pills that they killed their stupid selves. There's no crime here. Get back to work on some actual crimes."

On the desk between them was the empty box of codeine pills removed from the brass trash can on the barge by the sergeant after his post-piss discovery.

"But lieutenant, this box wasn't in the Brits' cabin and the prescription is for one of the other passengers!" exclaimed the sergeant. "I think they were murdered, and this empty box of pills will prove it!"

The lieutenant rolled his eyes. He lacked the resources to chase down real criminals. And now his sergeant wanted to take time away from real work to meddle in the deaths of a couple of Brits who probably did themselves in with drugs and drink.

It would be one thing if the deceased were French. But Brits? Who cares?

"No," he said again and, with a majestic motion, swiped the empty codeine box into his desk-side waste basket.

"Now, move on."

As the lieutenant turned his attention to his computer screen, the sergeant retrieved his evidence from the wastebasket.

Part Six

"I know who did it."

Jean-Claude looked into the unfocused eyes of the gendarme sergeant, the remnants of the gruel the sergeant had for lunch still crusted about his lips, his face unshaven, his hair a tangled, greasy mess.

"I know who did it," Jean-Claude said again but more slowly to hopefully assist the comprehension of the pitiful wretch in front of him.

The only person in France who cared about finding the truth was the gendarme sergeant now sprawled here. After months of dead ends and lack of support from his entire nation, he secretly provided information to the British in hopes that her leaders would have an interest in finding the killers of Brian and Hilary, if indeed there had been some killers.

It was not a secret for long. There was a leak to the news media, of course, and the effort by the sergeant backfired spectacularly as his fellow countrymen and women viewed him as a filthy traitor and they could care less about the meaningless demise of two unknown Brits.

The newspapers kept stoking the fire because it sold newspapers and was excellent internet clickbait. The whole mess became inflamed beyond reason. It was too much for the sergeant, and he slipped down a rat hole of insanity.

"I know who did it!" the sergeant was quoted by a newspaper accompanied by a full-page photo of him being escorted from the station house by two of his colleagues, one on each arm, his feet dragging on the cobblestones, a crazed look in his eyes as he was taken away to be incarcerated in the *Académie française des aliénés*.

Jean-Claude was fearful that his visit to the *Académie* was wasted. The imprisoned sergeant tried to flail his arms but they were constrained by a strait jacket. He furrowed his brow as if to use every smidgen of his withered brain power to understand what on earth this handsome man was saying to him.

Jean-Claude didn't know what to do. This man might be beyond help and might be incapable of helping to solve anything, including how to eat and poop. Jean-Claude looked around to see if any of the guards were looking. They were not.

He slapped the sergeant smartly across the right cheek.

"Come to, old man, I need you to think!" he commanded to the nearly incoherent sergeant who did not respond at all to being assaulted.

The young lawyer looked at the beleaguered sergeant with abject frustration and wondered if all his efforts were for naught. In frustration, he tucked his business card into the sergeant's shoe and left the *Académie*.

He had become enamored with the case of the dead Brits. Not that he liked the British people whom he viewed with the same dismissive disdain as the Irish and the Scots. These were a people who still thought they ruled the world, and they didn't. But, as a Frenchman, he had grown increasingly dismayed at the lack of interest his government had shown in solving the crime.

He also had a nagging thought that he might be involved, not directly of course, but perhaps as a witness. He acknowledged to himself that he wasn't much of a witness. He didn't really see much on that dark night on the canal, and certainly couldn't positively identify the miscreants if they were marched in front of him with their hair on fire.

But he was a man of justice.

And he had to take matters into his own hands.

"Madeline, my dear," he looked into the eyes of his delectable lover, she of the odiferous exhalations, "it is time we move on."

They were lunching at the Grand Hotel la Cloche in the heart of Dijon and feasting on an exquisite sole that was preceded by an elegant charcuterie tray paired with a splendid local white burgundy.

"What did you say?" an astonished Madeline asked, a piece of green something stuck in her teeth marring her otherwise classic beauty. A drop of snot escaped her nose and hung on her upper lip.

She was stunned. Normally when Jean-Claude drove from Paris and invited her to lunch at a local hotel, their dessert would be a frolic in one of the elegant rooms, a naughty diversion which she enjoyed immensely.

"What the fuck do you mean it's time to move on?" she demanded, raising her voice to a level that drew attention from the other patrons who were shocked at the words coming from the mouth of such an elegant beauty. If they only knew that the vulgarity was the nicest thing that ever came from that mouth.

"Well, my dearest..." Jean-Claude began.

"Don't you 'my dearest' me, you worthless piece of sheep shit," the lovely Madeline spewed, softening her profanities in consideration of their luxurious surroundings. "I demand that you tell me what on earth is going on!"

The dignified but horrified maître 'd moved cautiously toward their table, a veteran of calming irate diners, drunks and lovers who were suffering through a breakup or a spat of some kind or were just drunk.

"Good afternoon," he said, "may I assist you in some way?"

"Fuck off," Madeline hissed at him. "We'll be quieter. Get out of here."

The maître 'd did as he was instructed and quickly retreated to the safety of his podium where he hoped the next guests he seated would be more well behaved.

"Madeline, sadly but happily, I have found someone I like better," Jean-Claude said with a classic and dismissive French shrug of his shoulders.

Madeline stood from her seat, seething in anger.

The entire dining room watched with joyous anticipation to see what was next.

First, she threw her napkin at him then poured a glass of elegant burgundy over the top of his handsome head. She reached for more ammunition, but the other glasses were empty and a water glass lacked the drama of its wine brethren.

Jean-Claude remained in his chair, stoic, waiting for the storm to pass, licking what he could of the expensive wine as it dripped down his face.

"I hope you choke on one of those little bones in that ostentatious fish you love so much," Madeline said, hovering over him, close enough that her breath was making him nauseous. "You've taken the best months of my life and now you're casting me aside for someone else! I bet it's not even a woman! Or even a human!"

With that, she removed her shawl from the back of her chair and, with a practiced and elegant swirl, wrapped it around her enchanting shoulders with a flourish, turned and strode head held high from the dining room as the other diners whispered and giggled.

Jean-Claude, now sauteing in French wine, waited calmly at his seat. The maître 'd offered a soft towel to dry off, which Jean-Claude accepted with grace. He watched the drama of Madeline's exit from the dining room. When she was gone, he produced his smartphone from his jacket pocket and sent a four-word text to his new lover.

The phone vibrated discreetly.

Its owner was in a meeting with her colleagues to decide whether to prosecute the members of a French cycling team who had been terrorizing tourists for months. They traveled at excessive speeds through the country's beloved rural and quaint villages, speeds that had eventually led to a massive collision in a small town with minor injuries to a group of Danish visitors who had innocently gathered along the curb outside a bakery.

The hapless tourists were unceremoniously mowed down by a dozen cyclists on outlandishly expensive bikes. The riders were dressed in matching tightly fitted outfits and traveling at such high speeds that a conflict with anyone in their way was inevitable.

It was clear that the arrogant and high-handed cyclists could be charged with speeding but that was a local matter and not one that should take the time of the top attorneys at the country's *Ministère Public* in Paris.

However, one of the Danes was a constitutional expert who unearthed an archaic French statute that suggested that the offenses of the cyclists constituted anarchy and terrorism since they caused harm to innocent, foreign civilians where none should have occurred.

So, Allison Gravits was here with her colleagues in the attorney general's office for a decision-making conference to decide what to do about these two-wheeled terrorists.

She took a moment to look at her phone.

"The deed is done," it said.

She smiled and felt flush. It felt nice.

The text was from her new lover, a charming man named

Jean-Claude who was eight years her junior. She enjoyed the thrill of being with a younger man, the energy and vitality and enthusiasm he brought to their relationship, especially the physical part.

Allison had never had a boyfriend, or really any man who showed any interest in her. She spent all of her time working on behalf of the French people from her opulent office just down the hall from the country's top law enforcer.

She was fairly plain, she admitted, but she also acknowledged that she had a terrific figure that no man ever noticed because of the bland, formless business suits and casual clothes she wore.

Jean-Claude had noticed.

Their first date was her first date. Ever. She tried to dress provocatively, but failed. She could've worn a grocery bag and it would not have mattered to Jean-Claude. She had other attributes that interested him.

It took three dates before she would consent to come to his apartment for the night. He was an expert, experienced and creative lover, but she might as well have been a lifeless bean bag who had no idea what was going on.

He didn't mind.

He was playing a long game.

As they lay in bed after the fifth date, he finally concluded that enough time passed for him to make his move.

"Darling," he said, "I need a favor."

Oh shit," she thought, *here it comes. I knew it was too good to be true.*

"Anything, my dear," she replied sexily, touching his crotch.

"Well," he continued, pushing her hand away "do you recall the British couple who was found dead in the canal near Palinges a while back?"

"No," she answered coldly, wondering where this was going.

She stretched, luxuriating in the sensually exquisite delight of being naked in a huge and wonderful bed.

"It's understandable you don't remember," Jean-Claude blathered on, ignoring the naked woman next to him who was squirming like a cat in need of a belly rub. "But it's that calamity that was in the papers briefly and caused a mild kerfuffle with the British because our government didn't work very hard to solve it"

"Uh, so why are we discussing this in our bed?" Allison asked, squirming a little more, lightly brushing up against him, trying desperately to change the subject.

"I've become obsessed with it," Jean-Claude admitted. "I want to try to solve it. And I need your help. Professionally."

Allison sat up in bed. She looked at the love-tousled Jean-Claude and wished they were using their mouths right now for anything but jabbering about this rubbish.

She sighed, deeply.

"And just what do you possibly need?" she asked wearily.

"I'm not sure, but I have may some information about the case that could be useful," he said.

He went on to describe the dark night in Palinges (omitting the part about the passionate and lovely Madeline) and what he might have seen and what he might have heard on the night the two Brits were dispatched.

"So, let me get this straight," Allison said, again wearily, "you might have been a witness to a crime or perhaps the disposal of the bodies, but you couldn't see anything and you're not sure what you heard."

"Yes, dear, that's correct," he said.

She flopped back onto the bed in dramatic and exaggerated fashion. She felt certain that he had wooed her and bedded her to get something she could provide other than her warm body.

She felt used, but did a quick calculation that the drained satisfaction she now felt was probably worth it.

"What do you want?" she asked tersely.

"I want your office and your investigators to help me find four alcoholic Americans."

PART SEVEN

FOUR MONTHS LATER

TREY WAS on Gregg's doorstep, his iPad in hand.

Unlike Gregg, Trey's technology was world class and worked everywhere, even when he was out of sight of his home.

"Have you seen this?" Trey asked, shoving the iPad at Gregg.

Gregg took the device and quickly scanned a story reported by a London tabloid that apparently had been swirling through social media. Gregg might've been up to date on world affairs if his home computer was connected to the internet. He kept banging on the "enter" key, but nothing ever happened.

It was the story about the mysterious circumstances of the deaths of a British couple who disappeared while on a luxury barge cruise through the Burgundy region of France. The whole sordid mess had become an international scandal as the British government accused the French of ignoring the obvious murders of two of the Kingdom's citizens and refused to thoroughly investigate this horrible crime.

The tabloid gleefully reported how several Members of Parliament demanded that the Prime Minister dispatch without delay and with the utmost urgency one of the Royal Navy's most powerful and well-armed warships, preferably one with nuclear weapons if the Kingdom had such things, to the canal where this disgraceful incident occurred as a show of strength to the weak, pathetic and indifferent French people who thought about nothing more than the tangled histories of their beloved wines.

The Admiralty sent a firm but dignified missive to the delusional and moronic MPs that such an action would probably ignite another wasteful war between the two long-time adversaries. And, he added, the Royal Navy lacks any vessel small enough to fit into the canal except for perhaps a warship's lifeboat which would not send the type of threatening message to the recalcitrant French government that the ignorant MPs thought would be useful.

A source within the *Académie française des aliénés* also leaked to the tabloid that one of its inhabitants was the gendarme sergeant who had investigated the deaths but had gone batshit crazy and spent most of his days in a strait jacket screaming *"It was the damned alcoholics Americans, that's who!"*

Gregg looked at Trey.

"Is that us? Gregg asked.

"Duh," Trey said. "I'd say we're on the short list."

The story did not identify the alcoholic Americans accused by the deranged sergeant of the heinous crime, but it reported that the authorities in France and Great Britain kept looking for them and would certainly like to have a chat with them over a spot of tea or glass of white Burgundian wine if they ever stepped foot on British or French soil.

The words "detain", "interrogate" or "arrest" were never mentioned.

But it didn't sound good.

Gregg looked pale.

"Elisabeth and I are going to Ireland next month," he cried. "Does that count? Is that Britain? I sure don't want to end up in the Tower of London getting my head chopped off. I would look it up, but my internet isn't working right now. Or maybe it's my ethernet. Who can tell? What's the difference?"

"You think you've got problems," Trey said, panic and bile rising in his throat in equal measures. "Leeza and I are going to French Guiana next month and I don't know if that's really French or if they just stole the name. Who can figure this out?"

Gregg said, "While I've got your iPad, I'll look it up."

Trey grabbed his iPad away from his friend and clutched it to his chest, fearful that Gregg would accidentally touch a series of random keys that would render his device inoperable forever.

"You know what," Trey said. "We've gotten away with murder, literally and figuratively. It was entirely accidental, as we all agree. Let's just make sure we vacation from now on where they can't capture us."

"Excellent plan," Gregg said. "I'm glad you're thinking straight for a change."

Part Eight

Yet Another Month Later

"We found them," said the voice on Jean-Claude's phone.

"Who is we, and who did you find?" he asked.

"You asshole, this is Allison," she hissed angrily, "or had you forgotten that I existed and that you asked for a favor?"

"Excuse me," Jean-Claude said quietly to the young woman with whom he was enjoying lunch at the Café Dose Mouffetard. She was only sixteen and a summer intern at the law firm, but she had been open to his flirtations so he was on the prowl.

Jean-Claude stepped outside onto the busy street and returned the phone to his ear.

"It's been forever," he said. "I thought you'd forgotten *me!*"

He glanced into the Café Dose Mouffetard to check on his lunch date who was chatting with an infuriatingly handsome waiter and twirling her hair. *This call needs to be short.*

"How could I forget you, you dick," Allison hissed. "You broke my heart."

"It was in the name of justice," Jean-Claude decried gallantly. "Let's not bicker. Please tell me what you know."

Allison sighed deeply and loudly enough that Jean-Claude could hear it through his phone. He rolled his eyes. *Women.*

"What's all that noise?" Allison asked.

"I'm on the street. I am at lunch," he said.

"Whatever," Allison said, "go to your office and call me."

He swiftly reentered the Café Dose Mouffetard, tossed some Euros on the table, took his intern by the arm and escorted her out to the dismay of the aroused waiter.

Back at this desk, he returned Allison's call.

"You don't deserve this, you bastard," she said, "but the people of France do. Hell, if you solve this, you might get a knighthood from those British fools."

"I don't want that; I just want what you know," a desperate Jean-Claude said.

Allison then switched into professional gear and began a clinical recital of what the office of *Ministère Public* had accomplished in the case of the dead Brits.

She told Jean-Claude how her investigators (she omitted that they were junior trainees and didn't know what they were doing) patiently worked with the gendarme sergeant who originally investigated the crime.

"The big breakthrough," she said, "came when our little team coordinated with the doctors at the *Académie française des aliénés* to change the medicines being administered to the insane sergeant."

She said he briefly became coherent enough to provide some recollections of his investigation.

"And then you won't believe what happened," Allison said.

"What?", the excited Jean-Claude asked.

"The sergeant rummaged through his pitiful little bag of possessions," she said, "and handed the investigators an empty box of prescription painkillers.

"It matched the drugs found in the autopsies of the dead Brits. But time caused the name on the prescription to fade, so it was actually no use other than the contents were likely the cause of death. That plus several gallons of alcohol."

"Where does that leave us?" an increasingly irritated Jean-Claude asked. "What you're telling me is not helpful at all."

"So," Allison continued patiently, "we finally asked the barge company for a manifest of their passengers. I can't believe no one thought to do that. They resisted at first but then we threatened them with some legal nonsense, and they gave us the list.

"We identified the Americans who were on the barge that night.

"Then we used our secret resources – I could get fired for this, you asshole – to use their contacts at Interpol to set up a passport snare."

"What's that?" Jean-Claude asked.

Another deep sigh on the other end.

"A passport snare," Allison said wearily, "is an alert that notifies Interpol when someone on a wanted list uses their passport to enter a foreign country. Nothing happens at the border, but when their passport is swiped, Interpol gets a buzz and then whoever's looking for them goes to get them.

"The four Americans swiped their passports.

"And we know where they are."

PART NINE

AFTER SEVERAL DAYS at their resort relaxing on the beach and drinking cocktails with little umbrellas, the two American couples decided it was time to take a tour of the exotic island where they were vacationing.

They arranged a private car and a local guide to drive them around for a day that included stops at secluded and private beaches. At one of the beaches, an elegant lunch and a variety of wines had been arranged by a local restaurant and were served on the sand under a palm tree. It was extraordinary.

To make it even better, there was no cell service for most of the day, so no one could be disturbed. It didn't matter to Gregg, who hadn't had cell service since he pulled out of his driveway a week earlier. As the day drew to its satisfying conclusion, the two couples got into the little black van for the winding trip back to their luxury hotel where they hoped to arrive in time to watch the Caribbean sunset at a tiny tiki bar that faced the western sky and was famous for its sundowner cocktails.

The couples were thirsty for their upcoming cocktails and happily chatting about plans for another day on the sparkling beach as the van meandered through the island on narrow streets lined by picture postcard palm trees swaying in the gentle tropical breeze.

Without slowing, the van drove past the entrance to their hotel.

"Uh, excuse me," Trey said, whipping around his head, which made him slightly carsick after the lunchtime indulgences of excellent wine. "Wasn't that our hotel?"

The van sped up.

The driver and guide sitting next to him said nothing.

The passengers stopped talking and looked at Trey, who shrugged his shoulders.

"Perhaps they're taking us someplace for a special drink or something," he said.

They headed for the downtown area.

"Hey guys, what's up? We want to get back to see the sunset," Gregg said nervously.

More silence from the front seat.

The van came to a quick halt in front of a small cinderblock building.

It sure didn't look like a tourist spot or place to have a cool and comforting beverage.

It didn't look fun at all.

"Oh shit," Trey said, pointing to the sign on the building, "Look at that."

Turks and Caicos Government Headquarters
A Proud British Overseas Territory

Trey and Gregg gasped in unison.

"You're a total numbskull," Gregg said to Trey as Gregg jiggled the locked door handle trying to find an escape.

"Are you just going to leave us?" Elisabeth asked her husband as he desperately pushed against the unyielding door and jabbed at the window with his elbow, accomplishing nothing but injuring himself.

"If I can!" said Gregg, desperately still jiggling.

"Good gracious," Trey said. "I thought we'd be safe here. Who knew this was British?"

"Probably the entire world," said Leeza derisively. "What on earth is going on? Why are we here? What have we done?"

Trey ignored the questions.

The van door slid open, revealing a tall man in a military uniform, all sorts of medals and decorations on this chest, a sidearm on his belt.

"Welcome," he said, sounding like the villain in a James Bond flick. "We've been expecting you. Please, if you will, follow me."

The four passengers stepped from the van.

"Come with me," said the bemedaled tall man.

They entered the dark and smelly building and were guided to a tiny room with no windows, a small video camera with a blinking red light pointed at them.

"I was asked to have a spot of tea with you," said their well-decorated host.

Everyone held their breath. There was no tea. Gregg smoothed his hair for the camera.

"Our British overlords want to know if you remember Brian and Hilary," he continued.

"Who?" Trey asked.

Their uniformed captor smiled.

"You know very well who," he said menacingly, no longer smiling.

"I knew this was going to happen," Gregg snarled, glaring at Trey. "I read about this kind of stuff on the internet when I had a signal three years ago."

The tall man surveyed the terrified group in the tiny room. He slowly looked from one frightened face to the other.

"The alcoholic Americans," he said grinning. "I am so happy to finally meet you. I've heard much about you. And of all the colonies in the world held hostage by the British, you wandered into mine."

Nobody said anything. Nobody was even breathing.

The tall man then led them into a tiny room where a camera on a tripod faced the wall where a chart hung.

Mug shots.

Each of them was photographed, the women glaring at the camera as their heads continued to spin about what on earth was happening, the guys with sheepish looks.

The tall man, with the gesture of a doorman at an elegant hotel, directed them out of the little room and led them down the hall where he produced a huge key and unlocked a heavy steel door. When he opened it, the group could see it was the entrance to a row of jail cells. Leeza smacked Trey in the back of the head.

Each was locked in a separate cell.

"What have you stupid fuckers done?" yelled Leeza at Trey and Gregg from her cell.

"Yeah," Elizabeth said quietly. "It's confession time."

Trey ignored them. Instead, he shouted at the tall man.

"We have rights!" he yelled. "I demand a phone to call the United States Embassy!"

"You have no rights other than those I bestow upon you," said the tall man. "Besides, I didn't confiscate any phones. So, if you have one, you can call anyone you wish."

The only one of them who brought a phone on today's trip was Gregg, but he didn't have service as usual and hadn't charged it lately, so it only had 1 percent battery. The situation seemed hopeless.

Trey was trying to think of what to do next but couldn't concentrate because Leeza was dragging a tin cup back and forth across her cell's bars like she'd seen in the movies.

She paused her noisy disturbance briefly.

"Hey, Your Highness, does this place have a wine list?" she shouted, but the tall man had retreated so there was no answer, and she resumed her annoying tin can disturbance.

Trey thought he was going to scream and then the steel door opened. The tall man entered, unlocked Trey's cell and took him by the elbow out of the cell block and back to the tiny room where their mugshots had been taken.

"Sit," said the tall man, and Trey did.

"How much cash do you have," the tall man asked.

"Huh, what?" Trey sputtered and mumbled.

"You heard me. How much cash do you have?" The tall man repeated, "US dollars."

"Uh, I dunno, probably a few hundred dollars. Why?" Trey said.

"There are only two ways to resolve your little dilemma," continued the tall man. "One of them is to remain in this jail until I tell the British authorities that I've captured you and they give me direction on what do to with you.

"The other is in your control.

"Give me all the cash you and your friends have. As long as it is at least one thousand dollars, this situation will be resolved within moments."

"What will you tell the British government?" Trey asked, his voice trembling.

"You let me worry about them," he said with a huge grin. "They think they know everything and are masters of the world, but they're idiots just like those fat, dumb lugs who ended up dead in that French canal."

The tall man continued.

"I will return you to your cell where you and your fellow prisoners can count your money. You have fifteen minutes."

When Trey was back in this cell, he explained to the others what they needed to do.

The four alcoholic Americans looked at each other through the bars of their cells.

Leeza immediately dug into her purse, all the while glaring at Trey. Three hundred dollars and two wine corks.

Trey pulled four hundred from a secret wallet designed to deter pickpockets.

Gregg produced a small, black change purse like your grandfather carried. He dumped the contents on the table.

Thirty-seven cents.

Trey looked at him in disbelief.

"You're not serious," Trey said.

"That's it," Gregg said shrugging his shoulders.

"You mean to tell me that you have traveled to a foreign country with essentially no money?" Trey asked. "What were you going to do about tips and emergencies – as in the one we are in right now?"

"I have my Diners Club card and my Hechinger card," Gregg said. "I'm good."

"You idiot, nobody takes Diners Club and Hechinger went out of business three decades ago," Trey said. "And I don't think His Eminence in the other room takes plastic. You are definitely not good."

"Would you two idiots stop this nonsense and let's figure out how to get out of here," Leeza demanded.

They piled all their money on the table and counted it three times.

Seven hundred dollars and thirty-seven cents.

"Looks like serious jail time for us," Trey said.

"Wait, wait, wait!" shouted Gregg with uncharacteristic enthusiasm and energy. "I think I have a solution!"

"I bet this'll be good," Leeza said, rolling her eyes.

Gregg ignored her.

"I have billions in bitcoin!" he said excitedly. "I'm happy for us to use some of that to get us out of this fix!"

"Do you even know what bitcoin is?" Leeza angrily asked him. "Do you have some jangling in your pocket or in that little old man purse you just pulled out?"

"Well, to be honest, I've never used it before or tried to cash it or even how you get to it," Gregg said, somewhat dejected. "Apparently you need a working computer with lots of giga-something to get to your bitcoin, so that's always an obstacle for me."

Elizabeth, the quiet one in the alcoholic quartet, finally spoke.

"I have about a hundred dollars, which isn't going to help," she said. "But I have these."

She reached up to each ear and removed her earrings, sparkling diamonds in gold settings.

Elizabeth said sadly, "I'll happily donate them if it will get us out of here."

The four looked at each other, resigned to the fact that there was no other choice.

Trey banged on the door.

The tall man entered the room.

"Your Excellency, sir, we have an offer, part cash and part jewelry," Trey said. "Is that workable?"

The tall man moved to the table without replying. He ignored the cash and went directly to the earrings.

He held them up to the bare light bulb dangling overhead, and examined each one, turning them back and forth as they glistened in his fingers.

He stepped out for a moment, returning with a small magnifying glass which he used to continue his evaluation.

After several anxious moments, he slipped them into his jacket pocket and swept the cash off the table, pocketing it as well. He left the thirty-seven cents.

He then unlocked the cell doors one by one, took away Leeza's tin cup, and pointed to the large steel door.

"Get out of here," he said, a broad grin on his face. "There's a sunset awaiting you!"

Part Ten

Jean-Claude's flight was delayed and the line at customs was long and slow. A fight broke out near the front of the line that required police intervention. Something about bringing a live rooster into the country.

Then he got lost on the way from the airport.

He ended up on a dead-end unpaved street that looked dreadfully out of place in what was supposed to be a tropical paradise. He did a three-point turn in his rented Kia and, when he got turned around, the street was blocked by a Toyota pickup truck.

Standing in front of the truck were three men with handguns pointed at his windshield. Another was on the bed of the truck with some sort of long rifle.

One of them walked over to the window of the Kia where a terrified Jean-Claude pushed the button to roll it down.

"Give us everything," the armed man said, poking Jean-Claude in the nose with his gun, "including the car."

Jean-Claude reluctantly got out and handed the key fob and his wallet to the gunman. His suitcase remained on the back seat. He wondered what was next and whether this was his final moment to be alive.

"I said *everything*." the gunman said.

"I gave you *everything*," Jean-Claude said, worrying that his English wasn't keeping up with the situation.

"Your clothes."

"You've got to be kidding me," Jean-Claude said, nearly in tears.

"I'm not," replied the gunman.

Jean-Claude removed his shirt, trousers and shoes, leaving them in a pile on the dirt street.

"Those too," the gunman said, using his pistol to point at Jean-Claude's underwear.

Jean-Claude didn't react to the outlandishness of this request.

The gunman cocked his pistol and pointed it at the now shriveled-up nuts of Jean-Claude who immediately dropped his drawers and stepped out of them. He was now clad only in his silk socks with little garters around his lower legs to hold them up.

The gunman surprisingly ignored the smartphone in Jean-Claude's hand.

"Run," said the bad guy, and Jean-Claude did.

He dashed to the nearest main street and looked both ways, one hand covering his flipping and flopping well-used manhood and the other holding his phone, desperately using its GPS to figure out where he was.

In his current state of nakedness, he needed to get to his destination in a hurry.

He ran in the direction suggested by his phone, children on the street pointing, women on their doorsteps covering their faces, men laughing at his predicament. He kept moving, hoping his GPS would lead him to salvation and some clothing.

Woop woop

He turned. It was the siren of a small island police car following him, the red and blue emergency lights atop its roof blinking earnestly.

Jean-Claude stopped, defeated and deflated, head drooped in shame, a hand still covering his groin.

"What have we here?" asked one of the officers who emerged from the car, a huge grin on his face.

"Well, sir," Jean-Claude answered sarcastically, "you are looking at the victim of an armed robbery. Where were you when I was being robbed?"

The officer didn't reply as his partner brought a filthy towel from the trunk of the car and offered it to Jean-Claude who gratefully accepted it and wrapped it around his naked waist, holding it there with his free hand.

"The crime against you was witnessed by many," the officer said, "so we have been on the lookout for the unclothed victim. It appears we have found him. We are afraid of the gang that robbed you, so we will not look for them."

Jean-Claude stared at him in disbelief.

"So, what happens now?" Jean-Claude asked, straining to

convey his feelings in English.

"Where were you going before you were robbed?" asked the officer.

Jean-Claude quickly gave him an overview of his reason for being on the island and stressed the importance of quickly getting to the government building to help solve an awful crime.

The two officers looked at each other skeptically, unsure of whether this Frenchman was being truthful, was on drugs or was one of the crazy people who flee to this paradise is search of whatever.

"Get in, we'll take you there," the officer said, opening the rear door of the police car.

Somewhat unnecessarily but greatly appreciated, the officers turned on the car's siren and roared through the town's narrow streets and radioed ahead to the government house that they were en route.

They entered the parking lot too quickly, flinging gravel with great drama.

The sign on the building said:

Turks and Caicos Government Headquarters
A Proud British Overseas Territory

A tall man was waiting. He had many medals and an imposing firearm, which regrettably was not the first such terrifying weapon Jean-Claude had seen in the last hour.

"Who do we have here?" the tall man asked as the officers. "Why is this man not in handcuffs for the protection of all of us?"

"He's not under arrest but the victim of robbers who took everything except his pecker and his phone," one of the officers explained with a hearty laugh. "He said he had urgent business here."

"The most urgent business," the tall man said, "is to clothe this person. I shall not have an audience with a person who is naked. Take him inside!"

The officers hustled him inside where he was outfitted with an orange jumpsuit, the word *Prisoner* prominently featured on the back, and led to a small room with a camera. There was no red light, so Jean-Claude assumed it was turned off.

Moments later, the tall man entered the room.

"I would appreciate my previously naked guest explaining his visit to my world," he said.

"I am expected here," Jean-Claude breathlessly explained. "I am the one who called about the alcoholic Americans."

"And so you are," said the dignified tall man. "How may I help you?"

"I want to see them and have you arrest them. They are murderers!"

The tall bemedaled man went to a desk where he took a seat.

"You're too late," he said. "They have been released."

"What?" Jean-Claude asked in despair. "How did this happen? I thought they were to be held for several days!"

"Welcome to my world," said the tall man. "Circumstances changed. We reached, how can I say, an accommodation."

"But what about the British and French governments?"

Jean-Claude asked. "I thought their concerns would be respected!"

The tall man grinned.

"The concerns of those governments are of no concern to me," he said. "They may think they run the world, but they don't run mine."

Jean-Claude was crestfallen.

He had rushed halfway around the world to catch the Americans and have them arrested while they were on the soil of a British territory. And now this man with many medals, but apparently no sense, had let them go.

On top of that, he had been robbed and probably narrowly escaped death. He had no money, no passport, no toothbrush, no clothes or shoes, and not a single alcoholic American. What was he to do?

"What am I to do?" he asked the tall man.

The tall man stood, his medals clinking, his leather gun belt creaking as he adjusted it.

"I have a surprise for you," he said, an even larger smile on his face. "But, first, for my safety."

He moved behind Jean-Claude and quickly and expertly handcuffed him before he could resist.

"And now, your surprise," the tall man said with a big grin as he took Jean-Claude by the arm and led him to the exit.

It was twilight on a beautiful evening when they stepped onto the gravel parking lot of the cinderblock building where a minivan waited, its engine idling, the sliding rear passenger door open.

"You knew where to find the Americans," said the tall man,

"which meant the surprise awaiting you knew where to find you!"

From the other side of the minivan stepped Madeline and Allison.

The women moved around the car and stood on either side of the open sliding rear door; arms crossed menacingly.

Jean-Claude nearly fainted. They were very imposing and not nearly as sexy as he remembered.

He looked in hopeless desperation and fear at the tall man who tossed the handcuff keys to Allison, who missed the toss but picked them up off the gravel.

"They'll cut off my dick!" he pleaded to the tall man. "Save me!"

"Get in," Allison growled to Jean-Claude as the tall man forced him toward the car.

Madeline got in his face.

"Hello, asshole," she said, her breath triggering a wave of nausea.

With the tall man's help, the two women wrestled the struggling orange-clothed Frenchman roughly into the minivan, sliding the door shut with an authoritative slam. Allison handed a roll of US dollars to the tall man who smiled widely as he pocketed the money.

He waved as the minivan scattered gravel in its hurried departure, a muffled shout for help from within the vehicle.

Thank goodness all these crazy people are gone.

He paused for a moment to watch the sunset over the Atlantic, a soothing scene he'd witnessed countless times, but it seemed sweeter tonight.

Part Eleven

One year later

It was a quiet evening at the country club home of Gregg and Elizabeth. They were on their screened-in porch, the peaceful summer sounds of tree frogs and crickets croaking and chirping in the woods that encircled their home. Elizabeth was reading a book. Gregg was at a little table, his laptop in front of him. He had been pecking away for hours.

In the upper left corner of the laptop, it said "no service". The laptop screen was bright blue.

"Unrecoverable Error."

He didn't know what that meant, but was pretty sure he could fix it if he kept randomly jabbing at the keyboard. The machine was unresponsive so he decided now was a good time to take a break and he went into the house where he had hidden a gift for Beth.

He returned to the porch, a small bag in hand.

"What's this?" she asked with a smile as she took the bag, clearly excited and surprised because this was so out of character for Gregg.

She shoved her hand into the bag and retrieved a small jeweler's box.

"What have you done?" she asked sweetly.

Gregg just smiled.

She carefully opened the jeweler's box.

Inside were two magnificent diamond earrings in gold settings, nearly identical to the ones she sacrificed in the Turks and Caicos.

"I thought this was the least I could do to repay you for giving away your earrings on our trip last year," Gregg said. "You saved the day and helped us stay out of jail. They weren't insured, so I just paid for them. I wanted to make you happy."

Elizabeth stared at the earrings, speechless. It didn't seem to Gregg like she was as happy as she should be to have just received such an expensive gift.

"Wait here," she said, moving from her chair and into the house.

She returned with her own jewelry box and set it on the table.

It contained a smaller box, which she handed to Gregg.

He slid back the cover.

Two magnificent diamond earrings in gold settings.

Gregg stuttered.

"I don't understand," he said. "Where'd these come from?"

Elizabeth looked sheepish and was unsure of how Gregg

would react to what was coming next.

"These are my earrings," she said. "You gave them to me years ago."

Gregg was confused.

"But I thought you added them to the pile of bribe loot in the Turks and Caicos," Gregg said. "I don't understand."

"Nobody travels with their real jewelry, darling," Elizabeth said. "Those were travel earrings, fakes. That tall man on that little island has a pocketful of worthless plastic!"

"But why didn't you say something and let us know?" Gregg asked, calculating in his head how much he had now spent on two sets of diamond earrings. It was a lot.

"You boys had your little secret," she said, smiling sweetly, "and I had mine."

The buzzing of Gregg's cellphone interrupted their conversation. He held up the buzzing device and asked her which button would answer it, and she pressed it for him.

It was the security officer at the front gate of their club. A visitor was asking for them and requesting admittance.

"He's a very tall man in a uniform, lots of medals," the officer said a bit too excitedly. "He has a British accent and looks very important. He offered me a hundred bucks to let him in if I wouldn't call, but I couldn't do that."

There was an ominous click.

Gregg screamed into the phone. "Don't let him in whatever you do! He's here to kidnap us! Call the police and the sheriff! This is an emergency!"

Gregg looked at the phone. The battery was dead. He wondered if the guard heard anything.

"Elizabeth!" he shouted even though she was two feet away. "We've got to get out of here! Now! Our captor in the Turks and Caicos is here! At the front gate! He's gonna kill us for your dirty trick!"

"*My* dirty trick?" Elizabeth yelled back. "What about *your* dirty tricks that got us into the mess to begin with?

"We don't have time for this," Gregg said in a panic. "We've got to *go!*"

They moved quickly toward the garage. Elizabeth hoped that Gregg had remembered for once to charge their electric vehicle.

She sent a quick text to Trey.

"The tall man from the islands is here. Help!"

As they passed their large living room windows, the headlights of a car in their driveway flooded the room.

They both stopped and looked at each other.

Gregg knew he had to take action. But what? And with what?

He didn't own a gun. He tried to get a permit years ago but, for murky reasons that he never mentioned to anyone, the local sheriff denied his request. He ran into the garage, looking for a weapon, anything he could use to defend his homestead against this foreign, bemedaled invader with a grudge.

He saw his old golf clubs, but they were never any good at golf, so why would they be good weapons. Besides, they needed new grips.

Then his eyes landed on a legitimate weapon hanging on the garage wall, an old spearfishing gun from his days as a deep-sea diver. He'd never had the guts to actually shoot a fish with it, so it was brand new except for the numerous trips into a sea filled with brine and salt. He desperately looked for the spears. He wildly flung garage crap out of the way until he found one. He had no time to look for others.

This would be a one-shot opportunity.

He loaded the spear into the gun, barely remembering how, and noticed that the action seemed more sluggish than he remembered. No time for that, he thought, and raced back into the house.

The doorbell rang.

Gregg and Elizabeth clung to each other, terrified of opening the door and terrified of what would happen if they didn't. Gregg hid the spear gun behind his back and moved to the door.

The doorbell rang again, and then again.

He opened the door quickly.

"It's *you!*" shouted the tall man, pointing at Gregg with a smile on his face.

"It's *you!*" shouted Gregg in a high-pitched, girlishly panicked voice.

Gregg quickly moved the speargun to his shoulder and cocked it.

The tall man's smile evaporated when he saw the fearful looking weapon pointed at his bemedaled chest.

"But wait ...!" the tall man yelled, the palm of his right hand extended in front of him.

Gregg pulled the trigger. It didn't move.

Nothing.

A moment of tense silence.

The tall man was stunned that he was still alive.

Gregg shook the speargun, trying desperately to make it work. He had no Plan B.

He aimed again and pulled the trigger. Again, nothing.

The tall man moved swiftly to the front door, grabbed the speargun from Gregg and tossed it into the bushes next to the porch.

Gregg's shoulders slumped. Elizabeth was shaking with fear.

The tall man stepped back away from the front door and the terrified couple.

He raised his hands like a country preacher.

"Why such an angry greeting?" he asked, laughing and smiling. "I'm not here to harm you! I am here to bring you joy and make you happy! And you were going to kill me! Is that any way to treat a foreign dignitary? By the way, I have diplomatic immunity, in case you were wondering."

Gregg and Elizabeth looked at each other, unsure of what was going on. The tall man took a step forward and held out his hand. In it were two diamond earrings.

Elizabeth's worthless plastic.

"I am here at the request, or more accurately, the insistence of my government to return your property," the tall man said proudly, his bemedaled chest poked out. "My government regrettably obtained information, including despicable secret videos, that I was requiring bribes from practically everyone who entered our tiny island. In order to keep my post and all my medals, I was ordered to return the possessions of those who bribed me.

"So, here I am."

Gregg stepped forward and took the earrings. The tall man rubbed his hands as if washing them.

"What about our cash?" Gregg asked meekly, getting an elbow in the ribs from Elizabeth, the look on her face telling him to leave well enough alone.

"Just between us, I've kept most of the cash because the government had no idea how much I'd received and I don't know where most of the people are," the tall man admitted with a beaming smile. "I don't recall how much you paid me and, if I can't remember, it must've been such a paltry sum that it hardly matters. You have your jewelry. Be happy!"

And, with that, the tall man saluted and did a crisp, military-style about-face, and left their porch.

Suddenly, bright lights flooded the front of the house.

Blue and red flashing lights lit up the neighborhood.

Men in dark jump suits with automatic rifles and the word "SWAT" emblazoned on their chests emerged from the bushes and from behind the large pines in the yard, approaching with caution their tall target who thrust his hands high in the air.

"That's him!" shouted Trey from the safety of the darkness. "Shoot him!"

"What's Trey doing here?" Gregg asked Elizabeth, who shrugged her shoulders.

The SWAT guys moved forward, weapons ready.

"Why don't you shoot him?" Trey pleaded from the bushes. "He's an international terrorist!"

The flashing lights and all the racket had alerted Gregg and Elizabeth's neighbors, who emerged from the bushes separating their homes, each with a freshened cocktail in one hand, weapons in the other.

Will had an ancient shotgun breached to show he meant no harm and lacking shells anyway. Janie had a tiny .22 pistol she kept in her car to ward off potential kidnappers waiting to snatch her in the parking lot of the Target.

"And what are y'all doing here?" Gregg yelled, exasperated by all the commotion and now he had to deal with Will and Janie whose regular cocktail party clearly had been going on for a while but now was interrupted by the evening's events.

"We're here to help," Will said slightly slurring his words as he dramatically and one-handedly snapped shut the empty shotgun without spilling a drop of his drink. "We're here for your safety!"

"Nobody's gonna mess with our friends," Janie added, sloshing her drink on her blouse. "Not nobody, not no how."

Janie shoved her little pistol into her back jeans pocket as she lost her balance and gracefully swirled to the ground, landing on her butt.

There was a sharp pop as the peashooter accidentally fired, its tiny bullet exploding from Janie's jeans and banging into a rock in Elizabeth's garden, where it then ricocheted in Gregg's direction. Its inertia was nearly spent by the time it thumped into the crotch of his jeans, his left testicle taking the brunt before the little bullet tumbled harmlessly to the ground.

"I'm shot!" screamed Gregg, his hand to his crotch, doubled over in pain, face white as death as his testicle tried to recover from the painful thump of the tiny bullet.

"Shooter!" yelled multiple SWAT guys, who instinctively

reacted to the shot by surrounding Will and Janie and pointing their assault weapons at them.

"Cheers!" Janie announced from her seat on the ground.

Gregg looked at his hands for blood but saw none and quickly realized that he was not actually shot.

"Never mind!" he called in a soprano voice, raising his hand.

The SWAT team confiscated the weapons of Will and Janie and concluded that any threat from the neighbors had been nullified. Will helped Janie up from her seat on the grass and they ambled arm-in-arm through the bushes back to their home, hoping that all this ruckus would die down.

The SWAT team then quickly returned its attention to the tall man.

They politely asked him to lie face down on the driveway, which he did. They spoke quietly with him for a moment, and then helped him up, brushed him off and stood down from alert, several of them shaking his hand.

"What's wrong with you guys?" screeched Trey. "Take him out! Snuff the mutha!"

The SWAT leader walked over to Trey.

"What is wrong with *you?*" the officer demanded. "Do you know who this is? Of course, you don't, or you wouldn't have called in a SWAT response tonight."

Trey didn't like where this was going.

"He's one of the Caribbean's most respected drug informants and responsible for more intercepts by our Coast Guard than nearly anyone," the officer continued. "What you did tonight was reckless, patently illegal, and we might've killed that tall man.

"Turn around!" the officer commanded to Trey, who was so stunned he started to run away but was easily caught by two very large and nimble SWAT ninjas.

The officer handcuffed Trey and loaded him into an armored vehicle. Gregg and Elizabeth watched this spectacle from their front porch, where they waved farewell to both the tall man and to their friend Trey who they could hear protesting his arrest from inside his armored confines.

"Poor Trey," Gregg said, "I hope they have wi-fi wherever they're taking him."

The tall man didn't leave. He returned to the front porch.

He stared at them for a moment before speaking

"You know," he said, "when you were in my tiny country, we didn't even talk about what happened to those British fatties and who did it. Frankly, I didn't care. But I knew all along it was you alcoholic Americans.

"I figured you did the world a favor, so I gave you a lifetime of sunsets. I hope you always think of my kindness when you enjoy one."

With that, he jerked to a rigid attention, saluted, turned and walked away into the darkness.

As he approached the end of the driveway, the tall man abruptly stopped. He walked to the armored vehicle, its engine idling in the street, blue and red lights blinking in the darkness, its incarcerated passenger yelling frantically to be freed.

"Sir," said the tall man, snapping to attention and addressing the SWAT commander, who was on the phone to his superior trying to explain the nonsense that had just occurred and how many of the government's resources had been wasted.

"What?" the commander asked in exasperation. "I'll call you back," he said into the phone.

"Sir, I respectfully request that you release your prisoner," the tall man said with great dignity.

"Request denied," replied the commander bluntly.

"Sir, please reconsider," the tall man continued. "The captured individual meant no harm. None of these people knew that I was here to make recompense for the wrong-doings in which I engaged when they were guests in my tiny country."

"Where is this going?" the commander asked impatiently

"Well, sir," the tall man said, bowing his head, "I would consider it an honor if you would let him go. He made a mistake by raising the alarm, but not a criminal one."

The commander thought about it for a moment. Indeed, there would be paperwork galore that would take most of the rest of the night, not to mention court dates and depositions and testimony and all that other tedious mess that contributes to American justice.

"You got it," the commander finally said, pulling his keys out.

The tall man saluted sharply and faded into the darkness.

The commander unlocked the armored car door. Trey tumbled out, looked around, and moved toward his friends who were still in their yard.

They embraced, relieved that this night of terror was at an end.

"Well," said Trey to his friend Gregg with a laugh, "I guess we got away with another one."

"Whatdya mean *we?*" Gregg asked with a sneer.

Part Twelve

At that moment, at a regional airport, a jetlagged, scraggly and unkempt passenger emerged from a flight from JFK where it connected after a long flight from Paris. The flight was four hours late landing.

He still wore the identification wrist band from the *Académie française des aliéné* and scraps and cuts on his leg were all that remained of an ankle bracelet that he sawed off just minutes after his escape from imprisonment. The mind of the gendarme sergeant had been enveloped in darkness and confusion after the failed investigation into the deaths of the British couple.

But, one day it cleared like the morning fog on a mountain morning. Suddenly, he was completely lucid and understood who he was, where he was, and what he needed to do. He vaguely remembered a visit to his imprisonment by a fancy lawyer from Paris, a man who kept saying, "I know who did it!"

The sergeant still had the business card of the handsome visitor. He now had the names and addresses of the alcoholic Americans from the barge.

His escape from the *Académie* was simple and had been more like a casual departure than an escape because the guards were unaccustomed to clear-minded and cogent detainees and routinely left the doors unlocked. And he had passed with surprising ease through the border controls in Paris and New York in spite of his shabby appearance and ghastly body odor.

And now he stood in the choking humidity just a few miles from where he would find the alcoholic Americans, a few miles from where he would bring them to the justice they so richly deserved and for which the world at large needed.

They will not get away with this, he thought to himself as he waited for a cab.

The cab dropped him at the address he'd been given. He approached the door and rang the bell, which had a little camera in it.

"What do you want?" came a voice through a speaker in the bell, a technology the gendarme sergeant knew nothing about.

He leaned down to speak into the doorbell.

"I'm here to speak with some Americans," he said in his broken English. "Their names are Trey and Gregg. It is most urgent."

There was silence from the doorbell.

"Nobody here by that name," said the doorbell.

"But, sir," the sergeant said, "this is police business of the highest international importance."

"Then there's definitely nobody here by that name," the doorbell said. "You don't look or sound like no cop to me. Why don't you beat it before I call the real cops."

The sergeant concluded he had no recourse, so he retreated down the front walk of the house and back to the street. He looked at the house's mailbox. The number matched the one given to him by the handsome Paris lawyer.

I know the bastards are in there, he thought.

He looked both ways. This was an American suburb of which he was totally unfamiliar. There were no cabs in sight and he had no clue about an Uber.

He walked g down the street, spirits dashed, his mood sour, frustrated that justice had been delayed.

He walked for a while until he reached a small commercial area with a laundromat, a small grocery, a vape store, and a bar.

A police car was parked in front of the bar, backed into a space. He walked in.

It was dark, and he looked around. He went up to the bar and motioned to get the attention of the bored bartender.

"Excuse me sir," the sergeant said in his French-laced English, "do you know where I can find the police officer whose car is parked outside?"

The bartender tilted his head toward the end of the bar and toward the restrooms.

"I wouldn't bother him right now," the bartender said solemnly.

The sergeant sat down on a bar stool to wait.

"You sit, you drink," said the bartender.

The sergeant was briefly taken aback.

"Ok, Aperol spritz, s'l vous plaît," he said.

The bartender looked at him with contempt.

"That ain't a drink," he said. "Order something real. And order in English, dammit."

The sergeant thought for a moment, but his mind was blank.

"A beer, doesn't matter what," he said finally and the bartender returned with a Heineken, probably the most expensive choice.

The sergeant placed a twenty Euro bill on the bar.

"What the fuck is this? Play money?" he asked angrily.

Before the sergeant could explain, a police officer emerged from the restroom, adjusting all his equipment. He waved to the bartender.

"Excuse me officer," the sergeant said excitedly, "can you help me?

The officer stopped.

The sergeant produced his French police credentials, which did not impress the officer.

"This fucker tried to pay for a beer with phony money!" the bartender yelled. "Arrest his ass!"

The officer put up his hand to shush the bartender.

"What's the problem, sir?" the officer asked.

The sergeant explained that he was on a mission to find international criminals who had murdered British citizens in his country, and he was very close to finding them. He explained how he went to their address today and was rebuffed.

"So you were," said the officer skeptically. "Let's go to my car."

The sergeant was seated in the cage in the rear of the car while the officer tapped away at his computer. He tapped and tapped. He asked for the sergeant's passport which was provided.

He tapped some more, then spoke some codes into his radio. He kept tapping.

Finally, he stopped tapping.

"So, sergeant," the officer said. "you have the right address. But you're in the wrong town."

The sergeant leaned forward. "What?"

'Yeah, buddy, you're in the wrong town," the officer said, laughing. "A street with the same name is in every town in this state."

The sergeant flopped back in his seat. *Now what?*

"Let's go downtown," the officer said.

They arrived at a solemn looking government building and the officer drove his cruiser into a basement where he parked and opened the door for the sergeant, whom he put in handcuffs.

"What's going on?" the sergeant demanded, squirming as the officer cuffed him.

There was no answer from the officer as he led the sergeant into the building, down a long brightly lit hallway and into a small room.

"Wait here," the officer told him, and shut the door.

The sergeant waited for a couple of hours. It was just like being in the *Académie française des aliéné* except with handcuffs instead of a straitjacket. And not as clean.

Finally, a key rattled in the door and two new officers entered.

"We are from the United States Homeland Security," one of the them said. "We understand you're an escapee from the Academy of Something or Other. I can't pronounce it but you're supposed to be there and not here. So, you're under arrest."

The officer explained that the alert of his departure from the *Académie* had trickled through the world's passport system so slowly that he was in the US before the system could catch up, thus the ease with which he sailed through the sophisticated customs of two countries.

"And now you're going back," the officer said.

The anguished sergeant pleaded with them that his mission was most urgent and that murderers were on the loose.

"I must be allowed my freedom to find these alcoholic Americans!" he cried.

"Yeah, whatever," one of them replied.

The sergeant was escorted to a boarding gate where an Air France flight was preparing to leave for Paris. He was handed off to a French federal agent and, by prior arrangement, was held at the gate until all other passengers had boarded.

At the last minute, the gate agent motioned to the sergeant's escort that they could board, and they walked down the long jet bridge toward the awaiting aircraft. The lead flight attendant met them at the aircraft door and checked their tickets and seat assignments which were on the last row of the plane next to the toilets.

All the other passengers were settling in for the long flight. Those in first class already had their champagne and Bloody Mary's to complement those they had enjoyed in the opulent lounge inside the terminal.

As the sergeant and his captor passed through the first-class cabin enroute to the rear of the plane, he heard a voice, a familiar voice, a voice that caused his brain to explode with the vivid memory of a night on a barge on the *Canal du Centre*.

A southern American twang that he'd heard before.

"I've got a great duck joke that I'll tell when we get in the air. But I'll need two more of these Bloodies if I'm gonna tell it right."

He stopped in the aisle, resisting the pull of his escort.

Desperately he looked around the cabin, wide-eyed and crazy.

And there they were!

The alcoholic Americans!

They were drinking and clinking their glasses in a series of gleeful, excited toasts.

"It's them!" he shouted to the alarm of his escort, trying to twist free. "Let me at them! They're the killers of those British people!"

The first-class cabin fell quiet at the disturbance. They were concerned that this was a hijacker or terrorist or, worse, a commotion that might cause the bar service to be suspended.

"Hmm, I wonder what this is all about?" Trey nervously asked his wife and friends, each of whom shrugged.

Suddenly, from the coach section rushed a large man, a badge held high in one hand and a pistol pointed at the ceiling in the other.

"Air marshal!" he yelled as he moved toward the disruption.

The gendarme's escort held up his hand.

"Please sir," he said in broken English as he produced his own badge and credentials, "this man is my prisoner who I am returning to France where he belongs."

The air marshal holstered his pistol, relieved that this was not an actual terrorist event or hijacking, but concerned he had revealed his secret status to all the passengers.

"Si, señor," said the air marshal, speaking the only foreign words he knew. "Qué pasa, amigo? Qué hora es?"

The French escort spoke fluent Spanish and was momentarily confused why the air marshal needed to know what time it was.

"Sir," he replied, "it's time to go. Please help me place my prisoner in his seat."

Meanwhile, the sergeant had grabbed the folding door of the onboard toilet with his handcuffed hands, desperately trying to free himself from his captors so he could arrest the alcoholic Americans, visions in his twisted mind of his handcuffed hands around their alcoholic throats.

A brief struggle ensued, requiring the strength of both officers to yank him loose.

"I'll get you!" the sergeant shouted crazily in his heavily accented English as the two officers dragged him down the aisle. "You alcoholic Americans will be mine one day!"

Along with all the passengers, Trey heard this shouted threat.

He thought about it for a moment

No, you won't, he thought to himself with a smile.

When the aircraft reached its cruising altitude, he ordered another drink.

"Let's hear that duck joke," he said.

THE END

Author's notes

The nonsense in this book is the third iteration of this tall tale. This one was written with the intent of providing more depth and background about the story's hateful protagonists, to poke fun at them and to make my friends laugh. Of course, it got completely out of hand.

The first version was written for laughs on a smartphone on the sun-splashed deck of M/V Finesse, a hotel barge that was creeping along the Canal du Centre in southern France after my wife and friends had reached the end of our ropes with a British couple who were fellow passengers. Their behavior inspired the story. The second iteration was a slightly longer version included as a free bonus at the back end of my new novel *Smokes*.

My normal cadre of proofreaders and reviewers were mercifully excused from duty for this book. I couldn't bring myself to ask Lisa Piercy, my wife and the first set of eyes to read my stuff, to read these silly pages even though I am certain she would have. My sister Kay and her husband Nate also would have read it if asked, but I know they have better things to do (namely Mav and Zoe). Likewise, Barbara Reining surely would have agreed to read over my shoulder, but that would have distracted her from reading actual literature.

This book also corrects a mistake that appeared in the previous two novels where I copied and pasted the Author's Notes that said I lived in Pinehurst with "this" wife instead of "his" wife as if future wives are contemplated which, of course, they are not. Fortunately, his wife has a good sense of humor.

As always, I am appreciative of the patience and guidance of Kimberly Daniels Taws, the proprietor of The Country Bookseller in Southern Pines, NC, who is always willing to wipe the dust off the stagnant books of mine on her shelves to make room for more non-sellers that I bring to her doorstep. I am relieved that she is not dependent on me to send her son to college.

This is my fourth book with the team at Firebrand Publishing led by Amy Cancryn and am always amazed at how they can turn my rough and tangled mess into a professional book that makes me proud.

As always, the excitement and enthusiasm of Anne Piercy about my latest book is contagious and inspires me to begin another one.

ABOUT THE AUTHOR

Gene Upchurch is a native of Durham and a graduate of the University of North Carolina at Chapel Hill.

He was a sportswriter before embarking on a three-decade-long career in public affairs, community relations, and legislative advocacy in the utility industry. He is a proud recipient of the Order of the Long Leaf Pine, the State of North Carolina's highest civilian honor.

His previous novels, *The Eno Club* and *Burnt*, have not been international bestsellers nor was his first collection of short stories, *Vanessa*. Book purchasers have yet to fling money at his latest novel, *Smokes*. Hope springs eternal.

He lives in Pinehurst, North Carolina, with his wife, Lisa.

9 781941 907719